# The Year Nick McGowan Came to Stay

## REBECCA SPARROW

Alfred A. Knopf

New York

*Library of Congress Cataloging-in-Publication Data*
Sparrow, Rebecca.
The year Nick McGowan came to stay / Rebecca Sparrow.—1st American ed.
p. cm.
SUMMARY: In her final year of high school in 1989, Australian teenager Rachel has her world turned upside down when the most popular (and disturbed) boy in school comes to live with her family for a semester.
ISBN 978-0-375-84570-3 (trade)—ISBN 978-0-375-94570-0 (lib. bdg.)
[1. High schools—Fiction. 2. Schools—Fiction.
3. Interpersonal relations—Fiction. 4. Australia—Fiction.] I. Title.
PZ7.S73748Ye 2008
[Fic]—dc22
2007020758

Printed in the United States of America
April 2008
10 9 8 7 6 5 4 3 2 1
First American Edition

*For Brad,*

*the beetroot on my hamburger*

PROLOGUE

Rumors started going around about Nick McGowan pretty much as soon as school went back. Some people said he'd tried to overdose on sleeping pills and that his best friend in Middlemount had found him slumped over in his car and been forced to give him mouth-to-mouth. Others said he had to have his stomach pumped. That he'd left a note asking to be buried in his Dire Straits T-shirt. And that under no circumstances was anyone to play anything by Bette Midler or from the movie *Beaches* at his funeral. Kate Winter, one of the pretty boarder girls who hung around in Nick's group, who had the physique of a greyhound and a fondness for heavy black eyeliner, told anyone who would listen that the rumors were crap. She'd seen him over the summer break—gone and seen *Cocktail* with him at the Emerald

Cinema. New Year's Eve marked the anniversary of Mrs. McGowan's death, she said while teasing her strawberry blond bangs to within an inch of their life. So the Christmas holidays were always hard for Nick and his dad.

Back then I wasn't sure what happened to Nick McGowan the summer before we started our senior year. What I did know was that he went from being the first Year 11 student to top every subject to the first prefect to be stripped of his badge. And kicked out of the boardinghouse. On the night of the swimming carnival, at eleven-forty-five, Nick McGowan got out of bed, changed into his school uniform and systematically set off every fire alarm in the boys' boardinghouse. They eventually found him sitting on the Chapel steps—in clear view of the principal's house—smoking a pack of Benson & Hedges and doing his German homework. When Mr. Tallon, the principal, asked Nick what he was doing, he said that he had a German quiz the next day.

And that's when the PTA was called, my dad got involved and my troubles really began.

**ONE**

I'm staring at an egg timer, and for the first time in a week I'm wishing it would hurry up. That the sand would fill just a little faster so that I could have an excuse to get off the phone.

"Are you even listening to me?"

*No.* "Yeah, yeah. Zoë, you have two minutes."

"How can you even tell? What does two minutes of sand even look like? This is very Bradyesque. Didn't Mike make the Brady kids time their phone calls using an egg timer?"

"It was a pay phone. He installed a pay phone into the family room. Zee, I'm really—"

"Your parents seriously come up with the most bizarre punishments. You know, I think if my parents

3

found me making a one-hour international phone call, they'd just be happy that I was at home. As my mother says, if she can see me, it means I'm not out somewhere getting pregnant or doing drugs. You know, she's started subtly trying to check my arms for track marks. She keeps saying she's looking for moles, but I know what she's doing. She thinks I'm a teenage crackhead waiting to happen. I think she's been watching too much *Degrassi*."

"We have about a minute. Hurry up. Say whatever it is that you rang to say."

"Okay. *Pleeease* come to the party. *Pleeease*."

"What? We talked about this today. No less than an hour ago, outside the school gates. I've already told you I'm *not* going."

"Just for an hour?"

"No."

"Just for *half* an hour?"

"No." I nestle the cordless phone into my shoulder, take off my shoes and start to unzip my maroon uniform. I'm tired, and the last thing I feel like doing is having this conversation about some lame party in two weeks' time. I've got homework to start. It's week 2 and I already have three assignments. Welcome to Year 12.

"But you said that 1989 was going to be the year you loosened up a bit, let your hair down—became a bit more social."

"No I didn't."

"Well, you should've. And it's ridiculous for you not to be there when everyone else from the play is going. Even the stage crew."

"Why is Sally even throwing that party now? I mean, *Lady Windermere's Fan* all happened at the end of last year—we should have had a cast party then, not now. Not three months later."

"Well, she couldn't have it then because her parents wouldn't let her, but now they've gone to New Zealand and her older brother's in charge. So you've gotta come."

"Zee, you've known me since I was five. You should know that once I make up my mind, that's it. *I am not going to the party.* I've got assignments to start. This is a big year, and I plan to stay *focused* and work *really hard*."

"Who starts work on their assignments in week two? I swear, sometimes it's like you're a thirty-five-year-old trapped in a seventeen-year-old's body."

"Well, that was a waste of ten seconds."

"God, you're in a cranky mood."

"I'm tired, Zee. I just walked in the door. My feet hurt. And in an hour I have to go and be perky in front of fifteen four-year-olds. . . . Dad!"

My father's face has suddenly appeared at my door.

"Rachel, when you're off the phone, your mother and I would like to talk to you about something."

I nod. He leaves. I feel my face drain.

I turn back to the phone. "Ohmygod. They know."

"Huh? Why are you whispering?"

"Geez, Zoë. I said, *Ohmygod. They know.*"

"No they don't. You're being paranoid."

But all I can think as I hang up the phone is, *We're dead.*

# TWO

I knew there was trouble when I saw the chocolate cupcakes. In our house the appearance of chocolate is a sign. A bad omen. A jinx. A red flag that something bad is about to go down. In short, the worst moments of my life have all unfolded in the presence of chocolate-based desserts. In 1982 a plate of chocolate brownies appeared minutes before Dad casually mentioned that he'd accidentally thrown my Lady Di scrapbook into the backyard incinerator. In 1984 chocolate crackles were served as Mum announced that Caitlin, my younger sister, had accidentally taped over the episode of *A Country Practice* when Molly died. Before I'd had a chance to watch it. In 1987 chocolate mousse was on the table when Mum and Dad broke the news that I needed braces. And last year Mum had a chocolate Jaffa pie in the oven when Dad announced that his work conference in LA had been canceled. So instead of going to Disneyland for the school holidays, we'd be going camping. At Yeppoon. Again. Sensing our disappointment, Dad reached into his pocket and produced four tickets to *Disney on Ice.* I smiled and said it sounded fun. Caitlin said that she hoped Mickey slipped and that Donald ice-skated over his throat. She was a little bitter back then and, at thirteen, had the looks of a *Seventeen* model and the charm of Lizzie Borden.

So when I walked into the kitchen on Thursday evening and saw the plate of chocolate cupcakes on the table, the *Psycho* shower-scene music played in my head. I knew big trouble was brewing. I just didn't know what.

"What is it? What's wrong?" My fingers rap on the kitchen counter.

They glance at each other. My mind starts reeling, and I try to calm myself down. This could be about anything. A whole range of other bad news. Maybe Caitlin is returning home early from her exchange in France. Maybe they're about to get a divorce. Maybe I was adopted and my disarmingly hirsute birth mother wants to reclaim me and take me on the road as part of her Circus Oz act. Or. Or they *know*. In which case, I'm dead.

"So how *are* you?" Mum pats the seat next to hers at the kitchen table.

"Okaaay."

So they don't know about the enormous scratch on

the car. Haven't noticed the dodgy job Zoë and I did with the white car pen we bought from Repco. Zoë convinced me that the coloring-in would work since she did it all the time with the chipped wooden hat stands at CopperWorld. In both Zoë's world and CopperWorld there's nothing that a good bit of coloring-in can't fix. I look at my parents' faces. If they did know about the scratch, my mother wouldn't be quite this calm. Still, I have a horrible feeling about this talk. I think I'm about to get another "sex is about love" speech. Or maybe Mum's pregnant. I think I'm going to be sick.

"How's school going so far?" asks Mum.

I narrow my eyes. "Good."

"Still enjoying French?" she says.

"Yep."

*"La fourchette,"* says my dad slowly, as though he suspects I may be mildly retarded. "That's French for 'fork.'"

I turn and stare at my father blankly. I've been learning French since I was ten years old. I can debate the convenience of school uniforms, the importance of democracy and the reasons Australia should be a republic, all in near-perfect French. But in my father's head there exists the possibility that when it comes to *français,* I am yet to master cutlery.

And then Dad says, "So, Rachel, what we want to talk about is how you feel about Nick McGowan."

And before I can say, *Ohmygod, what is that supposed to*

*mean?* I'm listening in horror as my parents inform me that Nick McGowan, Nick "Oh, is that a fire alarm? Excuse me while I set it off" McGowan, Nick "sleeping-pill lover" McGowan, Nick "I only go out with girls who have the IQ of squid" McGowan, will be moving into Caitlin's bedroom for the rest of the year. And that I need to make him as welcome as possible.

"What? I'm sorry, but *what?*"

"There was a PTA meeting last night. Now, obviously Nick has broken the rules, and the school can't allow him to continue on as a boarder."

"Yes," I say. "That's right, because he's gone *mental,*" I say.

"Because he's had a tough time recently," corrects my mother. "Mr. Tallon explained to us that he's a straight-A student and a great boy who just happens to be going through a hard time."

I really, really don't believe this. I'm beginning to wish my strangely hirsute birth mother would show up. Circus Oz is beginning to look appealing.

"The school—together with Nick's father—has asked if any family might be prepared to let him stay with them," says my dad.

And there it is. My stomach drops.

"So, what? You put up your hand? Without asking me first?"

"We're just going to trial it for the first term. See how we all go," says Mum.

I look at my parents. "Do I get a say in any of this?"

"Well, it was a spur-of-the-moment decision," says my dad, glancing at Mum. "And it seemed like the right thing to do. We didn't realize it would bother you this much."

"Well, it does—bother me. It officially bothers me. I don't want him *here*. Living here. I don't want to get up in the morning and see *him*."

And for a moment I imagine what it would be like walking into the kitchen in the morning with my zits and bad hair to be faced with Nick McGowan's six feet of bad blond surfer looks.

"But you've always loved it when we've had exchange students come and stay. You got on so well with Tomoko and Johan. . . ."

"That's different, Mum. They're, they're . . . what's the word?"

"Foreign?"

"No. Naive. They were naive. I was able to convince Tomoko and Johan that I was cool. Nick McGowan isn't naive. I can't convince him that I'm cool—he already knows me. If you let him move in here, then you are giving me a whole heap more stress to deal with on a daily basis. And he's clearly lost the plot since last year. Something's snapped in his head. Do you really want me living with an emotionally unstable, suicidal maniac?"

"Rachel, I'd really feel more comfortable if you sat down and stopped waving the cake knife in the air."

I roll my eyes at my mother. "Fine."

I'm not getting through to them. I need to convince

Mum and Dad that this just shouldn't happen. I decide to go the academic angle. I point out that this is my final year, a year when I need to focus and a year when I don't need any distractions from my study.

But they've thought of that. Apparently. In what can only be considered as a shameless bribe, they're letting me move into the downstairs spare bedroom. Nick will move into Caitlin's room. So I get to have the downstairs spare room, which is much bigger and quieter. And it has its own bathroom. And air-conditioning. Hooray—but still, shit. *Shit.*

As a last resort I bring out the big guns. I lean across the table, look my parents in the eye and say, "Do you really think it's a good idea—nay, good parenting—to have two hormone-charged teenagers of the opposite sex living side by side?" Do I need to point out to them the skyrocketing rate of teenage pregnancies? Have they never watched *Blue Lagoon,* for godsakes? It's Brooke Shields and Christopher Atkins waiting to happen. Minus the turtles.

But my parents smile at one another and insult me further by telling me that they trust me completely. And as Dad ruffles me on the head, he says exactly what I don't want to hear—Nick McGowan is moving in on Sunday.

## THREE

An hour later and I'm standing in the back corner of a fast-food restaurant wearing a clown suit and getting fries pegged at my head by four-year-olds. This does not bode well. In a week's time I'm competing for the Party Hostess of the Year title at our restaurant. In one week I'm going head to head with Fiona Curtis—a Year 11 girl from some private girls' school who wears far too much puke-green. And, sure, I can acknowledge that Fiona's good. But she's no Rachel Hill when it comes to strapping on the clown nose and running a kid's birthday party.

And yet today, when I should be switched on, focused, in the zone, all I can think about is Nick McGowan. Not Simon Says. Not What's the Time, Mr. Wolf? Not Tiggy or Statues or Red Rover. Just Nick

McGowan and the fact that at some point soon it's fairly likely he is going to see me in my Fido Dido pajamas. And know that I like to eat tomato sauce on toast for breakfast. And be privy to the fact that because of a one-hour phone call to my sister in France, my phone calls are now monitored by an egg timer. For the next month I'm allowed to talk for no more than three minutes per call. To anyone. About anything. And Nick McGowan is going to know this—see the egg timer, be witness to my eggy humiliation.

I think about how much I want to ring Zoë to get her advice. And I look down at my big clowny thighs and think about how good it would be if I could lose weight before Sunday. And I ponder the fire alarm in the spare bedroom and wonder if Mum and Dad will take the batteries out before Nick McGowan comes to stay. And then I suddenly remember that I am supposed to be hosting Jamie Chapel's fourth birthday party. I suddenly remember because one of Jamie's friends—the one who smells like pee—tries to pull down my clown pants.

Someone yells out, "The clown has pink undies." Another kid yells out, "Petey pantsed the clown!"

I pull my pants back up, inwardly cursing the elasticized waist. Outwardly cursing Petey, who has caused me nothing but trouble since this party started. Petey who apparently wanted to play a game called Burn, Clown, Burn when he held a lit birthday-cake candle to my red nylon clown wig when I wasn't looking. Petey who—at the age of three and a half—wanted to know why if I'm a clown I have pimples. Petey who has now pantsed me no fewer than three times in thirty minutes. I briefly contemplate bashing Petey, but his heavily pregnant mother steps in and forces him to apologize.

"Sorry, Clown," he says.

"That's okay," I say, bending down to Petey's height, ruffling him on the head a little harder than is perhaps recommended by the Head Injuries Association. "So are you looking forward to having a new baby brother or sister?"

And that's when Petey looks me in the eye with the steady gaze of a serial killer and says, "When the new baby arrives, I'm going to put it in a sack and take it to see a dragon." And he says this with just a hint of kiddie menace. And then he skips away. Skips away, leaving me to clean up his cake plate and leaving his mother to contemplate joining a witness-protection program.

So far, today is not shaping up the way I had expected.

I look at my watch. Fifteen minutes to go. Fifteen minutes to go, and then I can go home and ring Zoë and figure out what the hell I'm going to do.

Then the faint but sickly smell of pee fills the air, and I feel two small hands pull down on my pants.

When I get home, I immediately ring Zoë, poised with the egg timer in my hand, ready to flip it over and talk faster than sand can fall. But Mrs. Budd tells me that Zee is on a theater excursion with her Drama class. They've gone to see *Hedda Gabler,* she thinks. At the Princess Theater. And the bus won't drop them back at the school till eleven p.m.

I put the egg timer down and drag my feet back up the stairs to my room. I ignore my lovely new desk and sit on the floor and start my French homework, but my mind keeps wandering away from my past perfect tense exercises and over to Nick McGowan. And I wonder what it will really be like having Nick McGowan living upstairs. And I wonder what he is thinking. Is he looking forward to coming here, or is he whining about it to the other boarder boys? *I can't believe I have to live with Rachel Hill's family—she sucks.* Was he hoping to get another family? Or is he pleased to be coming here to our house in Kenmore, where he gets his own room and lots of privacy and better meals?

I think about how I—along with every other girl in Year 11—had a sort of minicrush on Nick McGowan when he first came to our school last year. How there was that time in French when Mrs. Lesage paired us together to have a conversation about buying a train ticket for Bologna. How we both laughed about how stupid the cartoon fox was in our textbook and how if we went to France we'd just put *le* in front of every English word and hope to get by. But then he dropped out and decided to switch over to German, and we never really talked again. A month later I heard he was dating Kerry English, who was—of course—beautiful and popular and nice all the time and loved by everybody. And who, in Year 8, thought that babies came out of your bottom. But that didn't matter to Nick McGowan. Whenever I saw them together, it was always like they were sharing a private joke.

I look up at the full-length mirror nailed to the back of my bedroom door and contemplate my size 12 reflection. It pains me to realize that I look pretty much the same now as I did in Year 10. I turn my head one way, then the other, taking in my thick brown hair, my blue-gray eyes, my too thin lips, my too square nose and my too fat ankles. I know I'm not ugly. But I'm not gorgeous, either. I'm average. Ordinary. Plain. And sometimes I think that that's way worse. I think about Zoë for a moment, with her china-doll skin, her long, lean arms and legs and her mass of brown curls, which she, of course, hates. I overheard my mum once describe Zoë as "striking." *Striking.* Some days I'd give anything to be described that way.

For just a moment I imagine what would happen if when Nick McGowan moved in we fell madly in love. Imagine if I finally had a boyfriend. Imagine if we were the new "it" couple at school with our private jokes. What are the chances? Before I know it, I'm grabbing a pen and paper and I'm working out those chances. I'm writing out "Rachel Hill loves Nick McGowan" and I'm working out our Love Compatibility Score—the way you do when you're in primary school—by systematically crossing off the letters and then adding them up. We're 74 percent compatible. This cheers me up for some ridiculous reason. But then I look at it and see what I'm doing. This is ludicrous. So just to prove that it doesn't mean anything, I start working out my compatibility with all kinds of people. Kirk Cameron. Huey Lewis. Johnny Depp. Michael J. Fox. Each member of INXS.

My mum knocks, pauses and then opens the door, giving me just enough time to shove the pieces of paper into my homework diary and sit up at my desk.

My mother seems to get distressed when she sees me doing homework on the floor. "Are you all right down there?" she always asks, as though I was at the bottom of a skanky well and not sitting on 100 percent Berber carpeting.

"I have a cup of tea for you. You okay?"

"Yeah."

"This could all work out much better than you think. You might love having Nick McGowan live here."

"Mmmm." I shrug.

She smiles and nods hopefully. I smile back and say, "It's okay, Mum." She looks relieved. I thank her for the tea. When she's gone, I sip the tea in my favorite faded Holly Hobbie cup, put thoughts of Nick McGowan aside and concentrate on my homework.

FOUR

I don't sleep well on Thursday night. I dream that I'm
marrying Nick McGowan but that on the big day when
I walk down the aisle Martin O'Connell (a revolting guy
in my Drama class) is waiting for me instead. "I'm not
supposed to marry you," I say. But nobody listens. They
just keep going ahead with the ceremony, and I'm standing there knowing that I'm going to get divorced. And
how bad that will look on my résumé. Then I wake up.

On Friday morning I skulk into school, desperately
trying to find Zoë and even more desperately trying to
avoid running into Nick McGowan—or Martin
O'Connell, for that matter. But with a prefects meeting
at morning tea, I can't speak to Zoë properly about Nick
McGowan until lunch. We arrange to meet in the library

since Zoë has been cajoled into helping her aunt, the school librarian, restock some of the shelves.

In the ancient Greece section I grab her bony elbow, yank her away from a freckly Year 10 girl with red hair and start babbling to her about Nick McGowan and the PTA meeting and how, because of my dad and his big mouth, Nick McGowan is moving into Caitlin's bedroom for the rest of the year.

Zoë's reaction to my news is characteristically Zoë Budd. Her mouth falls open, her green eyes light up and she says, "This is great. You get to have sex with him."

So I hit her with my three-hundred-page *Web of Life* Biology textbook.

"I cannot *believe* you just said that."

"I can't believe you just hit me. I mean, think about it. You can lose your virginity in the comfort of your own home. Think about Lisa Staples, who did it with Gavin Piper out by Trudy Garrison's pool. On twigs and shit. No, this is much better."

I tell her that there will be no sex happening. Not now, not ever, when it comes to Nick McGowan. And that code name NM moving in is a bad, bad thing.

"What am I going to do, Zee? I don't want him living with my family. I don't want to have him reporting back to his friends on what goes on in our house."

She narrows her eyes, nods, purses her lips and then says, "Come with me." And Zoë drags me through the library, mumbling something about keeping your friends close and your enemies closer.

Ten minutes later I'm sitting at a library desk reading all about Nick McGowan. Zoë has found a copy of last year's *Boarder Review,* and in it there's a short profile on all the boarders—where they're from, what their interests are, their contact details. And it's a magazine that I've never seen since, as a day student, I don't get a copy.

"See? We need to find his Achilles' heel—his weakness—and then you've got something over him," says Zoë, perhaps a tad too enthusiastically.

So I sit there in the school library and read the paragraphs that have been written about Nick. About how he loves rugby league and cricket and Dire Straits and the Ramones and is well known for taking two desserts at the dining hall each night. Even on the nights they serve rice pudding. That his favorite film is *Beverly Hills Cop II.* His favorite TV show is *Simon and Simon.* That what he misses the most is his dog, Frank, back in Middlemount.

And then Zoë says, "Ohmygod, we should photocopy it."

And I say, "Yeah." Because this seems like a good idea. A good idea for me to have this info on file so that I can refer back to it whenever I want. Remember that he likes rice pudding. And ham-and-pineapple pizza. And dogs.

At the photocopier Zoë is feeding in ten-cent pieces like a crazy woman playing the slot machines, but the page keeps coming out almost black and a little big, as though the *Boarder Review* was written for very old people who can only see words written in a seventy-two-point font. So I put my books down, dig around in my purse, pull out as many ten-cent coins as I can find and hand them over.

As the machine keeps spewing out black copies, I say, "It needs to be lighter" and "Reduce it by fifty percent. You're not reducing it enough."

Zoë says, "I don't know what the problem is. This copier worked perfectly this morning when I photocopied my boobs."

And just when I think the bell is going to ring and we're going to have to come back after school, Zoë says, "Perfect!"

She swings around and holds up our now perfect photocopy of Nick McGowan's profile just as Nick McGowan walks through the library door and over to the photocopier.

"Hey," says Nick.

"Oh shit," says Zoë.

"We're just photocopying," I say. "We're just photocopying some stuff for Zoë's aunt."

"Because she's the librarian. And she just wanted us to photocopy some stuff for a display about boarders," says Zoë.

"Yeah," I say.

"Yeah," says Zoë.

"Right," says Nick. But that's all he says.

I look at Zoë. She looks at me. We've gotten away with it. We're in the clear. Nick McGowan has failed to notice that what we were photocopying was him. His profile and his photo. Like stalkers. Stalkers who photocopy very badly.

"We're finished," I say, more to my feet than to him. "You can have the copier now." And I wonder if my hair looks as crap as I think it looks. And I try to look calm and still look like someone who'd be fun to live with.

Nick McGowan moves to the photocopier and I begin to walk past him. I can't believe that neither of us is going to say anything about him moving in with my family this weekend. Then he grabs my arm and says, "Hey!"

I spin around, and so does my homework diary. I watch it fly—in slow motion—out of my hands before crashing onto the library carpet. Nick McGowan immediately bends down, picks up the diary and starts collecting up the other scraps of paper that I'd shoved inside. Scraps of paper, including one that says "Rachel Hill loves Huey Lewis." The note with the love heart. And the 81 percent rating. The note that I shoved into my homework diary when Mum brought in a cup of tea last night.

*Ohmygod.*

Nick McGowan looks down at the note, then at me, then back down at the note.

I say nothing.

Nick says nothing.

Zoë says, "I thought the rule was that you had to use the person's proper Christian name?"

Finally, Nick says, "Do you listen to Huey Lewis and the News?" And he says this with tone.

I just stare at him. Like a deer caught in headlights. A deer with bad taste in music. A deer that perhaps at one time wrote a fan letter to Huey claiming that he did indeed have "the power of love." And all I can think is, *Shit. Shit!* This is really, really bad. Now he thinks I like Huey Lewis and the News. I mean, I did listen to Huey Lewis and the News once, but I don't anymore. And I want him to know that. I just want to *die.* I look at Zoë with eyes that plead, *Ohmygod, help me!* But Zoë has whipped out a pen and is busy reworking the love percentage using Hugh instead of Huey. So I snatch the note from his hand, shove it into my dress pocket and say the only thing that comes to mind: "I've got a boyfriend, actually."

*I've got a boyfriend?*

Zoë looks up. Her expression makes it clear that my best friend is a little shocked at this confession. "You've got a boyfriend?"

I glare at Zoë. And despite the fact that she has no idea where this latest blatant lie is going, she says in an authoritative tone to Nick McGowan, "She has a boyfriend. And if he knew you were standing this close to her, he would beat the hell out of you. He's a little possessive."

"Right," says Nick. "And is his name Huey Lewis, perhaps? And do most of your dates happen on your bedroom floor with a picnic basket under his poster on the wall?"

Zoë laughs out loud. So I kick her.

"Very funny," I say. "As if I like Huey Lewis and the News." I snatch my homework diary and the other bits of paper from Nick McGowan. "This was a joke. I was trying to make my boyfriend laugh. It's just this little joke thing my boyfriend and I have. You know, we're always, um, laughing, and I wrote this out. It was a joke. You had to be there. Sort of."

Nick smiles. And nods. But I can tell he doesn't believe me. Then he says, "See you."

I feel my face go red. So I grab Zoë's arm and walk out of the library in silence and, when we're completely out of sight, turn to her and say, "I'm screwed."

## FIVE

I sit in French realizing how bad this situation really is. In the space of an hour I've been outed as a Huey Lewis and the News fan. And I've got an imaginary boyfriend. I think about the look of horror on Nick McGowan's face when he said, "Do you listen to Huey Lewis and the News?" And this is not the impression I wanted to create. I wanted him to think that I was cool. Instead, I look like a dork who is one fan letter away from a restraining order. I think about my room with its posters of Kirk Cameron and Johnny Depp and a-ha and Michael J. Fox and decide that this is *not* the way it's going to be.

Then I do something I've never done before. I tell Mrs. Lesage that I have a dentist's appointment and that I have to leave class early. And because it's me, Rachel Hill the prefect, Rachel Hill the good girl, she doesn't even ask to see a note. She just says, "Copy down your homework before you go."

"*Oui, madame,*" I say, scribbling into my homework diary. Then I pack up my things and collect my bag from the dayroom and stroll out the school gates an hour before everybody else, no questions asked. It's that easy.

Except for the bit where I don't actually know where I'm going. So I walk down Lambert Road and bypass my usual bus stop on Central Avenue and head for Indooroopilly Station. Fifteen minutes later I'm on a train to the city. On my way to Brisbane's coolest independent record store, Rocking Horse Records on Adelaide Street. On my way to get some posters for my room that will make me look cool. On my way to buy myself some street cred.

I find Rocking Horse Records easily. Not because I've ever been inside but because I've walked past it dozens of times with Mum when she was dragging me to McDonnell and East on the hunt for school-uniform supplies. But as soon as I step through the door, it feels like a bad idea. Me being here at two-forty-five on a Friday afternoon dressed in my deeply uncool maroon school uniform—complete with regulation maroon ribbon in my hair. There's loud tribal music playing that I don't recognize. I look around. I appear to be the only person in the room without a piercing. So I try to look like I fit in. After all, today I'm not Rachel Hill, prefect; I'm Rachel Hill, delinquent. Truant. Badass. Like someone who could possibly be riddled with piercings underneath all this maroon cotton-polyester mix. And I try to look nonchalant as I wander around the store flipping through CDs and records, fiddling with cassettes with no real clue of what the hell I'm doing. I even hum as though I'm familiar with the music that's playing.

I look over at the sales assistant, a guy with jet-black hair, piercings and tattoos. He looks like one of the bad guys in the "Say No to Cigarettes" commercials Ms. Michaels made us watch three billion times in Year 9 Social Education.

That's when I notice the young women next to me. One is dressed in army pants and a black tank top. She looks like Lisa Bonet from *The Cosby Show*, long dark dreadlocks, a pierced nose. The other has reddish braids and is wearing a long floral dress and Doc Martens. They look like uni students. I watch Lisa Bonet pick up a CD by the Housemartins, turn it over, put it back.

"Christ, this is the best album," she says to Braid Girl. Braid Girl agrees. Then they move to the *R* section—so I casually follow them. They flip through some CDs. Stop. Comment on how good the Riptides were in concert at the uni last year. Keep flipping. Then one of them says, "It's not here." The other says, "Go ask." Lisa Bonet goes to the counter and asks the guy if they have *Halfway to Sanity* by the Ramones.

The Ramones. Nick McGowan's Ramones.

"If it's not there, it means we don't have it," says the guy behind the counter. "We have it on cassette."

Lisa Bonet shakes her head.

"Okay, well, I can order you one in. You know their new one is out later this year? Do you want me to add your name to our preorder list?"

"Yeah," she says. "Thanks." I watch the sales assistant write down their details. Then Lisa Bonet and Braid Girl wander away, and I immediately know what I'm looking for.

Ten minutes later and I'm at the counter with two Ramones posters and *Halfway to Sanity* on cassette.

The sales assistant looks at my haul, then up at me.

"Bit of a Ramones fan, hey?"

"Fuck yeah."

He looks somewhat surprised. Then I hear someone go *tsk,* and I turn around to see a grandmother-type person shaking her head and clicking her tongue at me in disgust.

"Sorry," I say to the nana. And to the guy behind the counter. And to anyone else who heard me drop the f-word at 2:58 on a Friday afternoon.

"That'll be $28.31," says the sales guy a little suspiciously.

"Thanks," I mumble.

I hand over thirty dollars, sheepishly take my change and head out the door just as I hear the nana asking the sales assistant for directions to the Shingle Inn. As I walk back along Adelaide Street, I begin to cheer up. Today I'm a Ramones fan. And as I head back to Central Station, I can't wait to listen to their music.

**SIX**

I hate the Ramones. I spend Friday night listening to them and I make myself listen to every song on the tape. I find myself looking longingly over at my Bangles and Eurythmics tapes. Huey Lewis seems to be looking down at me from my bedroom wall with a look that says, *Traitor.* But I persist, telling myself that it's good for me. That I need to change. That I'm going to like the Ramones if it kills me.

By Saturday, listening to the Ramones nonstop has practically killed me. So I stop listening to them and instead I put on my Phil Collins *No Jacket Required* cassette (first lip-syncing in the mirror, "Billy, don't you lose my number") and resign myself to just memorizing the names of as many Ramones songs as I can. At least I can sound knowledgeable—look like I have something in common with Nick McGowan.

Dad walks past my door and reminds me that I can now officially move bedrooms. Caitlin is going to spew. We've been fighting over this room for years. Mum's always kept it as a guest room—mainly for my nana, who comes to stay from Sydney for a month every year. It's the ultimate bedroom. Bigger, quieter, away from the rest of the house. And, the pièce de résistance, it has its own bathroom.

I spend the rest of the morning moving my stuff. Books, cassettes, all my clothes. It takes me an hour to move all my stuff downstairs and another four hours to reinvent myself via my bedroom walls. I create a look that says Ramones lover, enigma, someone who's cool. And then Mum knocks on the door and asks if I want another cup of tea.

At one p.m. on Saturday I ring Zoë and invite her over for a swim and to look at my new boudoir. She arrives ten minutes later.

"Here it is," I say, ushering her into my new, bigger, air-conned bedroom.

I watch Zoë take it all in. I watch her eyes move from the bed to the bookcase to the posters on the walls. And then she turns to me, hands on hips and eyebrows raised.

"What?" I fold my arms across my chest.

"Since when do you listen to the Ramones?"

"I've always loved the Ramones," I say, perhaps not quite as convincingly as I would have hoped.

"Name one of their songs."

"'I'm Not Jesus.'"

"Really?"

I nod.

"Hmmm, okaaay. Then name two of their albums."

"*Halfway to Sanity* and *Animal Boy.*"

Zoë purses her lips and narrows her eyes, as though she suspects I'm wearing an earpiece and being fed the correct answers by some outside mole.

"What's the name of the lead singer?"

She's got me, dammit. I bite my lip.

"Umm . . . dunno."

That's when the penny drops. "This is the band that Nick McGowan said he liked. You're doing this to impress him. Nick McGowan. You're whoring your music taste to impress Nick McGowan!"

"Okay, fine. Maybe I am. But there is no way he was going to see the Kirk Cameron poster I had up in my room."

"Now just hang on a second. There is nothing, I repeat nothing, wrong with Kirk Cameron. That was a great poster. His eyes followed you around the room. I always felt like he was trying to hit on me."

"Oh God." I flop down onto my new double bed. "I'm screwed."

"You keep saying that."

"Well, it's true. Yesterday I made a complete dick of myself in front of Nick McGowan in the library."

"Sure," says Zoë.

I sit up. "You're not supposed to agree with me. You're my friend. You're supposed to say that things aren't as bad as they seem, that there's a solution here. That everything will work out okay."

I lie back down.

"But you made up a pretend boyfriend."

I sit up again. "I know I made up a pretend boyfriend. And thanks for your help, by the way. Your 'he would beat the hell out of you' contribution made it sound like I was dating Jack Nicholson's character in *The Shining*."

I lie back down.

"You know you're gonna have to find yourself a boyfriend."

I sit up again. "I *know*."

I stay up. I swing my legs over the edge of the bed and stare at Zoë on the floor. Zoë, who is currently balancing my Hello Kitty pillow on her forehead.

"The question is, What am I going to do about it? And take my Hello Kitty pillow off your head. You'll get makeup on it."

Zoë does her best horizontal volleyball spike and Kitty's fat little cat head comes sailing up toward me.

"Look, it's no biggie. All you have to do is break up with your pretend boyfriend some time next week. End of story."

"Right. Right. Of course. Break up with him. That's easy enough. I'll just casually drop into a conversation next week that Paul and I have broken up."

Now it's her turn to sit up. "*Paul?* Your pretend boyfriend is called *Paul?*"

"What's wrong with Paul?"

"It reminds me of Paul Fitch. Remember how bad he was at sports in Year 9? Remember how everyone used to call him Cerebral Paulsy?"

"Uh, no. I remember how *you* used to call him Cerebral Paulsy. And it was disgraceful. And—now that I think about it—you also convinced everyone to start calling me Ratshit."

"Sozzy," she says. "I thought we were going for a swim?"

"We will once Mum and Dad get out of the pool. How about Hamish?"

"Hamishhh. Hamishhh. It sounds like a rash."

"That's the dumbest thing I've ever heard."

"Oh, this coming from the person who once said the name Malcolm reminded her of a cucumber."

"That reminds me," I say, grabbing the piece of paper out of my pocket. "No cheese-and-onion sandwiches."

"Huh?"

"I'm making a list of ground rules for my parents. No cheese-and-onion sandwiches, no Mum calling me Pumpkin in front of him, no Dad coming to the breakfast table with just a bath towel wrapped around his waist. Ground rules, Zee. It's the only way I'm going to get through this year emotionally unscathed."

Zoë snatches the pen off me. And she starts to give me one of her famous lectures. She tells me that I'm panicking too much about this. That I'm acting like Nick McGowan is Johnny Depp or something. He is, she says, just some kid from Middlemount. I should take down the Ramones posters, tear up this list of ground rules and just be myself.

Naturally, I tell her she's wrong. The Ramones aren't going anywhere.

"Fine. But Nick McGowan is lucky to be staying here," she says. "He should be grateful. And your parents are about as normal as they come. Out of everyone's parents, yours are the best."

"They banned me from seeing *Fatal Attraction* when I was in Year 10."

"Rach, everybody's parents banned them from seeing *Fatal Attraction*. The point is your parents are—as far as parents go—pretty cool. They are *not* going to embarrass you."

I look up at Zoë, ashamed, and say, "You're right." I crumple up the list.

And then my dad saunters past the window wearing flip-flops, a straw hat and a pair of too tight Speedos. Too tight Speedos under a too big belly. He looks like he's smuggling his lunch down his pants.

Without saying a word, without even taking her eyes away from the window, Zoë hands me back the pen and I smooth out my sheet of paper to add rule 12.

SEVEN

I'm at work by eight on Sunday morning, and I'm
relieved not to be home at ten, when Nick McGowan is
due to arrive. I don't want to be there for those first few
awkward moments. I don't want to even know what
kind of hideous clothes my parents are wearing. Whether
my mother has lipstick on her teeth. Whether my father
starts to whistle or sing out loud like he does sometimes
in restaurants just to embarrass Caitlin and me. I'd rather
be here, working the fries machine, pretending that Nick
McGowan isn't possibly right this very minute becoming my new housemate.

My drive-thru shift ends at eleven a.m., but after
much pleading Chris agrees to let me stay at work, giving me a dining-room shift. So I spend eleven a.m. till
one p.m. at work filling the straw and napkin dispensers,

mopping up spills and peeling pickles off the artwork hanging throughout the restaurant.

At one p.m. I am still reluctant to clock off and go home. Nick McGowan will certainly be there now. Doing what? Unpacking his clothes? Looking through our family photos? Being made to sit through the holiday video of Yeppoon my dad took last year? I'm not ready to go back. Plus, I should really prepare for this birthday-party challenge. So I sit around in the crew room watching the American birthday-party training videos and taking notes. Fiona Curtis doesn't have a chance.

At three p.m. Chris actually orders me to go home. He says that I have watched the training videos enough times for today, that my behavior is bordering on obsessive. (This coming from someone who wants to go to Hamburger University.) I get changed and start the long walk home.

Technically, it's not such a long way. Today it takes me thirty minutes. Fifteen minutes of walking, and fifteen minutes hanging around outside the front door of my house trying to psych myself up for what awaits me inside.

I'm not good with change. From today onward everything is going to be different.

Deep breath.

Two steps inside the front door and the first thing I see is Mum and Dad and Nick McGowan standing in the kitchen—intervention style—as though they have been waiting for me to arrive. The second thing I notice is the plate of chocolate biscuits on the kitchen table.

## EIGHT

He gets my room. He's too tall for Caitlin's single bed, so he gets my room. My new bigger room with the air-con and the bathroom. My new cool room that I've lived in for less than a day. And now it's Nick McGowan's. I think about the fact that Nick has only been living with my family for three hours and forty-six minutes and already he's causing trouble. Wrecking things. Having me evicted from my new boudoir.

I sit at the kitchen table and chain-eat the chocolate biscuits while my parents serve up platitudes. They'll turn Caitlin's room into a study for me. They'll buy me a pedestal fan.

"But it wouldn't be fair to Nick to put him in a bed where his feet hung over the edge, would it, Rachel?"

I shrug.

Nick reaches across the table for the last chocolate biscuit, and as he does I slide the plate out of his reach. Then I give him a look that says, *Screw you, buddy. Screw you and your too long body. You can take my room, but you're not getting the biscuit.*

Mum says that I'm not to worry about how long it's going to take to move my stuff back. She's already moved my clothes and books back up to my old room. My old room with the faded clown wallpaper. I'm back to being the mayor of Clowntropolis.

"And I've put your Kirk Cameron and Huey Lewis and the News posters right back up on the wall, exactly how they were before."

I officially want to kill myself.

I look over at Nick, who is standing now. Nick dressed in a red polo shirt, baggy jeans with a battered brown belt and scuffed brown boots, his curly blond bangs hanging over his eyes in a manner that is blatantly detention-worthy. Nick McGowan who oozes cool. And he's standing in my house, my kitchen, staring at the floor, hands shoved in his pockets, biting his lip. Trying not to *laugh at me.* I feel like giving him a detention.

"I have Ramones posters on my wall. Those other posters were meant to be ironic. I've had them on my wall since I was little."

But nobody's listening. Mum has started asking if anyone wants a tea or coffee. Nick McGowan has started humming "Hip to Be Square."

Mum, sensing she's done something wrong,

something that may send her daughter into years of therapy, simply says, "Sorry, sweetheart. Well, why don't you go downstairs and move the last of your things up?"

"Like my Ramones posters," I say.

"Right," she says.

I don't look at Nick McGowan. I don't look at Mum or Dad. I just get up from the table and say, "I'll do it now. So Nick can have his room."

I hate this already.

# NINE

I stand inside the doorway. It doesn't even look like the room I left this morning. My clothes, books, lamp—it's all gone. My fingerprints have been erased. I'm back to how I was: a loser. And he never got to see it—the me with the cool bedroom. I step up onto the now stripped double bed and try to wiggle the first tack out of Ramones poster numero uno.

"I tried to tell them that I didn't care about my feet. You know, hanging over the side of the bed. For the record, I was prepared to sleep diagonally."

He's being sarcastic. I look over my shoulder, ready to shoot Nick McGowan my best withering this-isn't-funny glare. But he's not even looking at me. He's staring at the big photo frame that hangs above my bookcase.

The photo frame that Zoë made me for my birthday last year—full of photos of Zee and me over the years.

"You're best friends with that Zoë Budd?"

"Yep."

"You've known her since you were little?"

"Since I was five."

"You look close."

"We are."

His eyes slide away from the photo and over to mine. I immediately turn back to the wall.

Three tacks to go. I'm regretting hammering them in. I figure the key is to not rip the poster as I try and pull each tack out. Out of the corner of my eye I watch Nick McGowan reach out and touch the other Ramones poster above the desk.

"These posters look newish."

I stop, turn around with my hands on my hips. "What's that supposed to mean?"

Taken aback, Nick says, "Aah, it means these posters look newish. I'm just wondering if they're new?"

"Well, they're not *newish*. They're *oldish*. I happen to have liked the Ramones forever. And I've had these posters for a while. Up in my old bedroom for quite a while. Not that it's any of your business, but they're old, not new, they're old. O-L-D *old*, okay?"

I concentrate on pulling the last tack out of my "not new" Ramones poster, the poster that has allegedly been on my wall for a while, a poster that should therefore be well creased and rather limp. And as soon as I pull the last tack out, this poster commando-rolls itself up. Back into a cylinder.

Nick stares at the poster. I stare at the poster.

Nick says, "Define 'old.'"

I feel my face going red, so I turn back to the wall and pretend to scrape off old bits of Blu Tack. "Look, why don't you go and watch TV out there or something? I won't be long. Then you can move in."

I turn around to see Nick McGowan's reaction, but he's already gone.

It takes me half an hour to transform my old bedroom into something that isn't totally humiliating. I glare at the clowns and wish bad things upon them as I cover as many of them as I can with Ramones posters. "You're like a virus," I say to the clowns. "Some kind of freaky circus virus spread all over my walls." But the clowns just grin inanely back at me in return. "I'm not your friend!" I yell at them.

I start Blu Tacking my extensive a-ha and Johnny Depp poster collection back onto the walls. I think of Nick in the room below me. Unpacking his stuff. Putting his T-shirts and jeans and sneakers away. Looking around. Wondering how he ended up in downtown Kenmore.

I notice that in the midst of her earlier redecorating Mum has left the cordless phone on top of my bookcase. I decide to take the opportunity to ring Zoë.

I push the ON button and put the phone to my ear, only to hear that someone is already on the line.

An older, gravelly voice is saying, "This is not up for discussion, Nick. We're not talking about it anymore. I am not going to let you throw your life away."

Then I hear Nick McGowan say, "So what *I* want doesn't matter? I mean, maybe I just want to be in Middlemount. Maybe I'm just going to spend my life working in the mines—like you."

Just as I'm contemplating whether to hang up or keep eavesdropping, Mum calls out, "Rachel, the shower's free. Rachel?"

I quickly hang up. "I'm going now!"

"Don't be too long—and leave some hot water for Nick."

"Okay," I say, and I walk into the bathroom, trying to make sense of what I just overheard.

# TEN

It takes me a good ten minutes to find him. Having searched every room in the house, I eventually decide to look outside, down by the pool. I wander to the edge of the courtyard steps, steps that lead down to the pool area, my eyes leaning over the edge, skimming over shapes that could resemble a seventeen-year-old male.

It's the smoke that betrays him. He's sitting on the pool box—a big rectangular wooden box my dad made to keep the pool chemicals in. He's sitting on the box, down the back of our yard, smoking a cigarette. I walk toward him. I see his profile looking up at the night sky.

"Dinner is in half an hour. It'll be Kentucky Fried Chicken in front of the TV while my entire family watches *It's a Knockout*. You have thirty minutes to mentally prepare yourself."

I turn to leave, but his smoking is something that . . .

"You know, my dad will kill you if he finds you smoking."

"He knows."

"He knows? *My dad* knows you're smoking? Down here? Right now?"

"I told him I was going to come down here for a smoke."

"You told my father you were going outside for a cigarette? And he said that was *okay*?"

"I'm not sure he said it was okay. I think his exact words were, 'Well, Nick, I'd appreciate it if you used an ashtray.'" He gestures toward the faded Felix the Cat mug that Sarah Klein gave me for my thirteenth birthday. My father who once offered my sister and me one thousand dollars if we could make it to twenty-one without even puffing on a cigarette is now handing out ashtrays to other teenagers. A recruitment boy for Benson & Hedges. This makes no sense to me. But then nothing makes sense to me anymore. I turn back to Nick and look at his face, suddenly mesmerized by the way the cigarette nefariously balances on the edge of his lips.

"Are you going to try and get yourself kicked out of here? Is that your plan? Because maybe you don't care, but this is a big year. I was looking forward to having a quiet, non-eventful year. So if you're going to start, you know, setting off fire alarms, then could you let me know? Because I'm going to need to factor it into my study timetable."

He stares at me as though I have just spoken to him in Greek. "Are you always this uptight, or do I just bring this out in you?"

My mouth falls open. My brain shifts like a Rubik's Cube as I struggle to think of a comeback.

"Nick!"

We both turn. My mother is standing on the veranda waving the cordless phone at us. "There's a phone call for you."

"Jesus." Nick grinds his cigarette into the bottom of the Felix mug. "It'll be my dad. Again."

"It's a Sam Wilks for you," yells my mum, putting the phone to her chest.

I turn and watch Nick's tanned face turn deathly pale as he slowly gets up and goes to the phone.

ELEVEN

He's on the phone with Sam Wilks for half an hour. I offer to go and get him for dinner, but Dad looks at Mum and then quickly tells me to leave him go. Mum says, "We can start without him." She's going to leave a plate for him in the oven. No egg timer for him.

I start heaping chips onto my plate, and then I remember what happened down at the pool. I stop—mid–chip grab—and look at my father.

"Nick said you said he could smoke."

"Nick's going through a tough time right now, Rachel. And he's eighteen, so legally he's allowed to smoke, so . . ."

I didn't know he was eighteen.

"What tough time? I think I should know what's going on—just so I can be mentally prepared if I come home one afternoon and find him sticking his head in the oven."

Mum looks at me and rolls her eyes.

"Rachel, you're being silly. Nick is just dealing with a few problems at the moment. So you need to give him some space."

"That's not what they're saying at school."

"Well, you should know better than to listen to rumors."

"Well, why can't you just tell me?"

"Because it's not for us to tell you what Nick's been through. It's up to him."

"Fine."

So I slump into the lounge and do what we always do on a Sunday night at six-thirty—watch *It's a Knockout* (a lame game show on TV) and eat Kentucky Fried Chicken for dinner. It's the only time we're allowed to eat in front of the TV, because Mum says she's too tired to cook. And she happens to like Kentucky's coleslaw. So we sit there and watch TV, and my dad says what he always says every Sunday night: that the male host, Billy J. Smith, seems to be losing weight. And that Fiona MacDonald's teeth are so white, they remind him of the Osmonds'.

And I sit there and pray that Nick doesn't come down right now while my father has coleslaw on his chin.

During a commercial break I make an excuse to go downstairs so I can loiter past Nick's bedroom door and hear what's going on. And—of course—that's when he opens the door, wiping his red swollen eyes, only to find me standing outside. Staring right at him.

"What are you doing?" I watch as he rakes his fingers through his blond bangs to push them off his face.

"I was just getting . . ." What? I'm not sure, so I abandon this sentence by the side of the road.

"Are you crying?"

I pause. Decide to try another tack.

"Are you okay?"

"I'm fine," he says before running up the stairs two at a time.

"Define 'fine,'" I mumble as I follow up behind.

TWELVE

"Maybe it's his best friend, the one who saved his life."

I stand at the school gates trying to keep one eye on the uniforms of the students passing by me and one eye on Zoë.

"Nup. Mum pretty much said that stuff was crap."

"So your mum *knows*?"

"Apparently. But they won't tell me anything. Anyway, you didn't see his face. When Mum said the name Sam Wilks, Nick looked like he was going to spew. And the other thing I forgot to tell you is that Mrs. Ramsay, the counselor, rang him as well. He spent most of the night on the phone. Hang on a sec, Zee."

I go over to a Year 9 girl who has sauntered through the gates wearing her hair down. As soon as she sees me, she ties it back in a ponytail. I give her a look that says, *I'm watching you. And your hair.*

I go back to Zoë.

"*Ohmygod,* did you see how big her boobs were? She's in Year 9, for godsakes. She's gonna put someone's eye out with those things." Zoë looks down at her chest. "What the hell is wrong with the two of you? You're not even trying."

"You've been reading *Are You There God? It's Me, Margaret* again, haven't you?"

"Well, I read somewhere that if you name things and talk to them every day, they're more likely to grow."

"That's plants, Zee. *Plants.* Not your boobs."

"Oh, right, right," she says slyly. And then out of the side of her mouth she whispers to her chest, "Don't listen to her. Mummy loves you."

"You're a freak."

"I've got it!" she says, hitting me in the arm. "Maybe Sam is his dad?"

"No. Mum and Dad have spoken to Mr. McGowan. And plus his surname is McGowan, not Wilks. Mum wouldn't say, *Sam Wilks is on the phone,* she'd say, *Your dad's on the phone.* And anyway one of the conditions with Nick McGowan living with us is that he has to ring his father every Tuesday night. So Sam Wilks is not his dad."

"But maybe Nick McGowan is adopted. And maybe Sam Wilks in his *real* dad. His biological dad. Huh?" She nods enthusiastically. "His biological dad has heard that

Nick tried to kill himself and now he's ringing to check on him."

"You've been watching too much *Knots Landing*."

"You should have asked Nick this morning instead of racing off to get the early bus. You're an idiot. And another thing, you've got a hot guy living in your house and you're not making the most of it."

"And what would you be doing?"

"He's got the best body out of any of the guys in Year 12. So for starters I'd accidentally walk in on him in the shower."

"Yes," I say. "That's right. Because you're a perv. I'm just waiting for the day you ring me from prison asking for bail money. And haven't you got an early guitar lesson? Get going and let me concentrate on my job."

"Okay." Then she drops to her knees, grabs my hand and starts pleading. "Pleeease come to the cast party next Friday night. *Pleeease*."

"No."

"God, you're a stick-in-the-mud." She pokes out her tongue and says, "I'll see you at morning tea."

In the next twenty minutes I bust two Year 9 girls for wearing illegal black lace hair ribbons, a Year 11 girl for wearing her sports uniform, a goth Year 10 boy for black nail polish, and Simon Guilfoyle for trying—again—to walk through the gates wearing a hat. Despite the fact it's summer. And about seventy-five degrees. I don't enjoy busting people. I pride myself on being one of the nicer prefects. A shoulder to lean on, a big sister to come to in times of crisis. But I still have to give them all warnings or detentions. Rules are rules. And the school community has entrusted me to help uphold the image of the school. I'm not helping these students by letting them look messy, by letting them flaunt their hats in my face.

And then Nick McGowan strolls through the school gates in his sports uniform. And even though this is a detention-worthy offense, even though I busted someone just fifteen minutes ago for doing the exact same thing, I find myself turning my back and pretending not to see him.

THIRTEEN

The day drags. In Modern History Mrs. Finemore says that if we're well behaved, she'll let us watch a video about Stalin. Only at school is a Stalin documentary offered up as a treat for good behavior. As usual, most of the class fails to respond, except Jenny Hamilton, who puts up her hand and asks if it's the documentary that was on the ABC last week. And weren't we supposed to be doing a pop quiz today? Someone groans. Someone else throws a pencil at the back of Jenny's head. Mrs. Finemore doesn't notice or doesn't care—she has a headache. Again. She wants us to spend the first half hour reading quietly from *Crossroads of Modern History.* Again. So Stacey McMaster and I spend the entire thirty minutes writing notes to each other about Mrs. Finemore's dress looking like it was made out of a curtain.

Accordingly, we spend the rest of the lesson referring to Mrs. Finemore as DWT: Drapes With Teeth.

When the lights are dimmed and the video comes on, Emma P. and Meredith tap me on the shoulder and ask if it's true that Nick McGowan is living at my house. That they'd heard that he and I had to share a room. A bedroom. They smile conspiratorially at one another when they say this. So I find myself filling them in on the story so far. Even though I don't really like these girls, even though I wouldn't usually have much to do with them. As the words pour out of my mouth, I can tell that as soon as my back is turned, they're going to twist what I've said—pretzel my words, and turn them into something completely different. But right now I can't have them thinking that Nick and I are room buddies. When DWT starts to walk over to us, I turn back around and try to watch the film. But I find myself watching Mark Martin put pencil shavings in Jenny Hamilton's hair. Jenny doesn't even realize they're there until Stalin's third Five-Year Plan.

Through all of this my mind keeps going back to Nick McGowan and how I should have stopped him at the gates. Given him a detention like everyone else. I think about what he said on the phone to the man who must have been his dad. About changing his mind. And wanting to work in the mines. I'm sure it was Nick McGowan who last year got claustrophobic when the Biology class went on a field trip and had to crawl through some caves. So how the hell is he going to work in a mine? And everybody knows that Nick McGowan has been obsessed with becoming a doctor since he was eight years old. He's the only person I've ever met who's done the Red Cross first-aid course six times. When I was in Year 10 and felt confused about what I wanted to do, Dad took me to the careers center on Ann Street, helped me realize that there were lots of great jobs out there that would be perfect for me. Options—that's what Nick McGowan needs. Perhaps it's time for a brochure intervention. And perhaps if Nick McGowan was reminded that he doesn't have to choose between medicine and mining, between jobs that start with an *m,* he'd feel a bit better about school.

And that's when I come up with a plan.

FOURTEEN

"That's a shit plan."

I look over at Zoë, who is sitting on the edge of a table, swinging her long alabaster legs, crunching on a biscuit while she reads a brochure on town planning.

"Giving Nick McGowan brochures on different careers is not a plan."

"You know you're not allowed to eat in here," I say, gesturing to the NO FOOD OR DRINK sign in the library Careers Room.

Zoë rolls her eyes, shakes her head—which just succeeds in shaking her mass of brown curls—and says, "Always such a negative vibe. You're gonna have to work on that, Rach. It's not good for my aura."

"And it's not a shit plan. I think it's a good plan.

Maybe Nick McGowan is drowning, and maybe I'm the person who can help him. That's what I'm good at. I'm good at helping others. And in many ways I don't have a choice because it's in my job description, you know, as a prefect."

Zoë rolls her eyes.

"Blah, blah, blah. Good for you. You deserve a big pat on the back with something heavy. The fact is I can't believe that we've nearly spent our *entire* lunch hour in here trying to find a good career for Nick McGowan. I don't even know what *I* want to do next year." She sighs.

"I thought you were going to do Arts?"

"I told that to my dad and he said, 'No daughter of mine is doing an Arts degree.' He said it's a degree in nothing, won't get me a job. He thinks I should be doing Law. But that's just so he can go around saying, *My daughter's doing Law*. So I'm going back to Plan B."

"Which is?"

"Teaching. Hey, wanna come round to my place tonight and watch *The Sound of Music*?"

"You're joking, right? You know how much I hate that movie. And you always get annoyed when I start cheering Rolfe on to blow the whistle."

Zoë sticks her tongue out at me. I roll my eyes and keep searching for brochures. And while I try to think of careers that might appeal to an eighteen-year-old guy from Middlemount, Zoë lies down on the library table, closes her eyes and from time to time bursts into random falsetto renditions of "Edelweiss" and "Sixteen Going on Seventeen." I start to suspect she has *Sound of Music* Tourette's syndrome.

When the bell goes, I'm armed with fifteen brochures on different careers, a book on good study habits (for myself) and no clue whatsoever on how to give the brochures to Nick.

# FIFTEEN

At the bus stop after school I mentally rehearse how I could casually bring up in conversation with Nick McGowan the fact that I have some brochures he might like to look at. I decide to lead in with the idea that I was in the library looking for myself—or Zoë. Yes, he'd believe that I was looking for Zoë, since she comes across as directionless. I practice the conversation over and over like a newly recruited Avon lady preparing for her first door knock. I go over the scenario. Nick and I will be on the bus together, I'll say something witty to make him laugh. Then I'll casually mention that Zoë and I were in the Careers Room at lunchtime. And how I'd picked up some brochures that made me think of him. But not in a romantic way—in a flatmate kind of way. And he'll realize that I'm not uptight. And he'll be incredibly grateful. So grateful that he'll ask me to go rollerblading with him this weekend.

By the time the 303 bus rolls up, I'm feeling confident. Problem is that Nick McGowan is nowhere to be seen. So I find myself getting on the bus alone.

And doing my homework alone.

And setting the table for dinner alone.

I wonder where he is—I don't remember him saying that he had something on after school today.

"Maybe he's run away?" I say to my parents as I put the salt and pepper on the table. "It was probably the whole *It's a Knockout* thing last night—pushed him over the edge. If he wasn't suicidal before he came to live with us, a few evenings of people running around dressed in gorilla costumes should do the trick."

But my parents aren't listening. My mum is now folding laundry and my dad is engrossed in the news. Then Mum walks into the lounge and asks Dad, "Is it really necessary to have the TV on so loud or are you hoping to make us all deaf?"

She's in one of her moods where she sighs a lot and asks a lot of rhetorical questions. (Is she the only one capable of making the gravy in this house? Do the rest of us have broken hands?) These moods don't happen very often, but when Mum's had a particularly stressful day at work, I've learned to make myself scarce.

Once when she was folding the laundry and asking no one in particular, "What does it take to get a little help around here?" Caitlin made the mistake of thinking she wanted an answer and said, "I dunno. Maybe more pocket money?"

This was not the right answer.

On many, many levels this was not the right answer. Not in the least because Mum doubled our after-school chores for that week and halved our pocket money. Needless to say, Caitlin and I have since learned the meaning of the term "rhetorical question."

At six-thirty, just as Mum starts ferreting around in the drawer for a serving spoon, Nick McGowan walks in the front door.

"Nick!"

My parents greet him the way the regular barflies greet Norm on *Cheers*—like a long-lost friend, not a houseguest who is late, hasn't called, has had us all worried that he might have been avoiding coming home because he hates living here already.

"Sorry I'm, um, late." He pauses, bites the inside of his lip and looks from Mum to Dad to me.

"It's fine, Nick," says my mum. "You've got just enough time to have a quick shower if you'd like. I can keep this warm for another few minutes."

Then my mother winks at him. My mother, the woman I have been known to call Attila the Mum, is now winking at Nick McGowan like she's some hip, easygoing type of mum. *This is false advertising,* I want to say. *She's not usually a winker. There's no winking in this house. Ten minutes ago she was questioning whether her life purpose was to make gravy.* I watch my parents happily watch Nick wander off downstairs, and I'm tempted to ask my mother if she's also planning to roll Nick some cigarettes while she's at it.

I don't say much during dinner. Mainly because I'm worried that Mum's beef Stroganoff is overcooked and that Nick McGowan will notice. Or care. And then tell everyone at school tomorrow that the food at the Hill house is worse than at the dining hall. But instead Nick demolishes his meal, politely answers my father's questions about Middlemount and even goes so far as to ask my mother how she gets her mashed potatoes so creamy. (Milk and an egg, apparently.)

After dinner I get up, stack my plate on the sink, grab a green apple from the fruit basket and head for the stairs. I remind my parents to let me speak to Caitlin if she should ring.

By the second stair I overhear Nick McGowan thanking Mum for the "really brilliant dinner, Mrs. Hill."

By the third stair I overhear him offering to do the washing-up. I start bounding up the stairs two at a time. Too late. By the eighth stair my mother's said those fateful words: "Rachel can help you."

I turn, go back down to the fourth step. "No, see, Mum, I've got an English oral exam to prepare for. I really don't have time to—"

Mum walks to the bottom of the staircase, throws the tea towel at my chest and says, "The wok may need to soak overnight."

• • •

Nick McGowan and I are alone with a sink full of dirty dishes. In a weary tone I ask if he wants to wash or dry. He chooses to wash. I sigh loudly to convey the inconvenience of this whole exercise. Then I push the plug into the drain hole, turn on the taps and squirt some washing-up liquid into the water—just to get him started.

I pick up the scrubbing brush, and rather than give it to him, I point it at his chest.

"Just so you know, this isn't one of my regular jobs. I realize you were trying to be polite and helpful and all that kind of thing, but doing the washing-up after dinner completely screws up my study timetable. See, my mum usually does it. And right now"—I look up at the red kitchen clock—"between seven and seventy-thirty p.m., I'm supposed to be studying English."

He takes the scrubbing brush from me.

"So you really have a study timetable? And you actually *stick* to it?" His tone is incredulous, as though I have just admitted to having a tattoo.

"Yes."

Now it's his turn to sigh. "Of course you do."

"What's that supposed to mean?" I put the dinner plate I'm holding down on the counter. "What's wrong with having a study timetable?"

"Life's too short."

"To what? Study?"

"You don't get it, do you? Study, exams, school—it doesn't mean anything. That's what I've realized lately—

that none of that shit makes a difference. The sooner you get that, the better."

"You've completely lost your mind. Of course it matters. It matters if you want to actually get into university next year. Personally, I think it's pretty funny that *you* are trying to tell *me* that study isn't important. You who just so happened to top every subject last year. I mean, just because you've changed your mind about doing Medicine doesn't mean that next year you're not going to have to do a lot of—"

"Who told you I changed my mind about Medicine?"

Oh shit.

"Well, I just sort of overheard you talking to your dad on the phone the other night."

"You eavesdropped on my conversation?"

"No. Okay, well, yes, but . . ."

Ohmygod. I look at his face. He looks horrified.

"No, see, technically it was an accident. I picked up the phone to ring Zoë and—"

"First my dad and now you. *I don't want to be a doctor anymore.* Okay? Why is that so difficult for people to understand? Just because I wanted to do it for years doesn't mean I'm not allowed to change my mind."

"You don't have to bite my head off. And, whatever. Do Medicine. Don't do Medicine. I don't give a shit what you do."

"So have you taught Nick to play Best Free Feelings yet?"

Nick and I both turn and stare at my father, who has walked into the kitchen.

"I have to warn you, Nick, she's pretty good at it."

My dad looks at me and then at Nick, who understandably looks confused. "Scratching an itch is always a good one. Or finally getting to a toilet when you're busting to go."

*Ohmygod.* "Dad." I shake my head to indicate he should drop this topic. "We're not playing that. Will you just . . ."

But my father is clearly surprised by my lack of enthusiasm for the conversation at hand. "What? You and Caitlin always love playing that game," he says, throwing his hands up in the air. Then the penny drops and he says in a worried tone, "Was Best Free Feelings on the list?"

Nick immediately says, "What list?"

I turn and look at him. "It's nothing."

"The list Rachel wrote out of things her mother and I weren't allowed to do or say once you moved in," says my dad with a grin and a wink in my direction. "Rachel's worried we'll *embarrass* her. But it's fine, I'm not going to take it personally."

*Ohmygod.*

Nick turns to me. "You made a *list*? You actually *made a list*?"

*Ohmygod.*

"I'm also not allowed to sing in the shower or whistle in the car," continues my father in a jokey tone.

*Ohmygod.* "Dad!"

"All right, I'm going," says my dad. "Realizing that your hiccups have gone, that's another good one," he calls out over his shoulder.

My father now out of sight, Nick turns to me and says, "What on earth—"

"Look, my father has a habit of coming to the breakfast table wearing nothing but a bath towel around his waist—so, yes, Nick, I made a list of ground rules for my parents."

"And what's the hiccups thing?"

"Best Free Feelings is a game my family plays when we're washing-up on camping trips. But I don't want to talk about it. And I certainly don't want to play it right now with you."

"Fine."

"Fine."

"Well, just do me the favor of not eavesdropping on any more of my private phone calls."

"Fine. And *you* do *me* a favor and next time you want to suck up to my mother, volunteer to wash her car or something. I have my own after-school chores that I'm expected to do. And this"—I wave my arm at the sink and the now-full dish rack—"this *isn't* one of them. Okay?"

"Fine."

"Fine."

And we finish the washing-up in silence.

SIXTEEN

We develop a workable routine that succeeds in keeping us out of each other's way. I set my alarm every morning for 6:15, which gets me up and out of bed half an hour before him. And everyone else. Any time I have to spare before I need to leave for the early, early bus is now spent hiding things from Nick McGowan. I can't afford to give him any ammunition to start spreading stories about me at school. Yesterday morning I remembered that my Cher aerobics tape was sitting out—in full view—in the TV cabinet outside his bedroom. This morning I moved the ugly photo of Caitlin and me at my twelfth birthday party into the drawer in my bathroom.

As far as school goes, we seem to have an unspoken agreement to stay away from each other. If I enter the library and he's there, I leave. If he rounds the corner to the cafeteria and I'm sitting at a table with Zoë and Stacey, he leaves. It could be worse, I guess. He could have found my Cher aerobics video.

I'm preoccupied thinking about all of this during Monday's period 1—PE—while Miss Perkins is trying to teach us the finer points of archery. Not having listened properly to her instructions, I struggle to load the arrow into the bow. I look up just in time to see Emma P.'s arrow hit one of the outer, outer circles on the target. " 'S your turn, Rachel."

With the arrow in place, I lift the bow up, pull it back. Someone has their hands over my eyes.

"You've had sex with him, haven't you?"

"Shit! No!" I struggle free from Zoë's grip. "Keep your voice down."

"It's been a week! Come on, tell me you did the funky-funky with him over the weekend. In which case, I hope you used a condom because, frankly, a pregnancy is going to be a little difficult to hide in this uniform."

I wave Megan Howie through to have a turn while I deal with Zoë. "What are you doing here? Miss Perkins is going to see you."

She points to a group of students on the far side of the oval. "My Health and PE class is playing soccer. Just thought I'd pop over and say hello. So are you still V?" She does a peace sign with her fingers.

"Believe me, Zoë, when I lose my virginity, you'll be the first to know. But I haven't. For starters, I saw Nick

McGowan for, like, five minutes over the entire week-end. He had detention all day Saturday and all day Sunday as punishment for setting off the boardinghouse alarms. Mr. Tallon made him weed this oval."

Zoë makes a horrified face.

"I know. Other than that, the closest contact we've had was doing the washing-up together last Monday night and . . ."

"And he plunged his head in the sink and tried to drown himself in the washing-up water?"

"Zoë!"

"What? I'm joking." She rolls her eyes at me as though I've lost my sense of humor. Then she takes a Mars bar out of her pocket, peels the wrapper off and takes a big bite out of it.

"It is a mystery to me that you are as skinny as you are, considering the amount of shit you eat."

"Bite?" She asks this through a mouthful of choco-late, pointing the Mars bar in my direction.

"No thanks. He keeps to himself, Zoë. He arrives home every night just before dinner, and other than mealtimes he's either in his room listening to loud music or out by the pool having a smoke. We completely ignore each other. Anyway, my point is that I really don't think he did try to kill himself over the summer. He just doesn't seem suicidal."

"How does someone 'seem' suicidal?" She does air quotes with her fingers.

"Oh, I dunno. Depressed? Crying a lot? I don't

know. All I'm saying is that as far as the rumors go, maybe they're wrong. Maybe nothing happened."

"Yeah? Well, Stacey McMaster said she saw Nick McGowan talking to Pastor Mears after school last week. And Stacey reckons there's a passage in the Bible that says that if thou committeth suicide, thou shalt burn in hell for all eternity."

"I don't think 'committeth' is a word," I say, more to myself than to her. Miss Perkins starts walking toward us. I nudge Zoë to leave.

"Apparently, Miss Perkins still lives at home with her parents, and she's twenty-seven! What a loser!"

I push Zoë in the arm. "Go!"

She starts to walk backward across the oval, still talking to me. "All I'm saying is that people are saying that Nick McGowan might be a bit . . ." She spins her finger next to her head and makes a crazy sign. "He could be trouble."

Twenty-four hours later and I realize Zoë's right.

SEVENTEEN

I'm sitting in detention—all thanks to Nick McGowan. Nick McGowan who is sitting two rows behind me. I look around. Simon Guilfoyle sticks his tongue into his bottom lip, making a gorilla face at me. I don't belong here. I'm not one of them. This is loser central. And I'm a prefect, for godsakes. I'm supposed to be the one who hands out detentions. Most of the people here are here because of me. What's worse is that when I walked into the room, Ms. Michaels assumed I was looking for someone.

"What can I do for you, Rachel?"

I looked at her. I looked at the other students. I fixed my gaze out the window and forced myself to say, "I'm here. On detention. Mr. Verney gave me a detention."

Then she said, "Oh," in that obvious "I'm disappointed in you" tone. It was nothing short of humiliating.

Naturally, I tried to point all of this out to Mr. Verney, my Math in Society teacher, but he wouldn't listen. Mr. Verney had been in a bad mood ever since school started back. There were rumors that he was getting divorced, backed up by the fact that he'd suddenly started wearing inane cartoon ties, had grown a goatee and was spotted reading *Men Who Hate Women and the Women Who Love Them* in the staff room. So when I tried to reason with Mr. Verney, explain to him that I was a prefect and that Nick McGowan was to blame, Mr. Verney looked at me, then turned and continued to wipe down the blackboard.

"You and Nick have earned an afternoon detention like anyone else," he said, chalk flying up around him.

"I know that detention is like a second home to you, but you've gotta tell him," I said to Nick on our way out of Math in Society class. "You've gotta tell Mr. Verney that this is your fault. Not mine. I don't think you understand. I can't be on detention, Nick. I'm a prefect. What will people think? It will ruin my school record. Plus, I have a party shift at work at five p.m. I simply can't be on detention this afternoon."

Nick's response? He told me that none of this would have happened if I hadn't started behaving like a banshee.

So I told him he was an asshole.

So he gave me the finger and walked off. Nice.

• • •

Martin O'Connell farts next to me. This fart carries the stench of rotting food. For a moment I imagine a pile of putrid, rotting vegetables and chicken carcasses fermenting in Martin O'Connell's stomach. I feel like throwing up. I can't believe Anna Davis ever went out with him. With my hand covering my nose and mouth, I glare at Martin O'Connell, but he looks smug. Typical. So I turn left—in a bid to find fresh air—and watch what the students around me are doing. Some of the younger kids are writing lines. The older ones are just expected to do homework. Two girls behind me are discussing what happened to Dr. Terence Elliott in last night's episode of *A Country Practice*. But I can't concentrate in this environment. I'm still not sure how I ended up here. I go over—again—how events unfolded the way they did.

There was me, minding my own business in Math in Society. Then there was Nick, turning up at my Math in Society class out of the blue, telling Mr. Verney that he's decided to drop down to Math in Society from Advanced Math.

Mr. Verney looked Nick up and down and said, "Well, Mr. McGowan, you won't be joining us unless your parents sign a form consenting to the change. And there will be no more subject changes after this week. So you'll need to get it back to me by Friday."

"My dad's in Middlemount, sir."

"Well, you'll have to get your guardians to sign it."

Nick said that this wasn't a problem and that he'd get

the form signed. He glanced over at me and my gaping jaw and then boldly took the desk behind me.

Mr. Verney lent Nick a textbook for the lesson, and Nick sat in class and started behaving like he belonged there. With those of us who don't *get* math. But he doesn't belong. He *needs* to be doing Advanced Math to get into Medicine.

"What about your dad? What about Medicine? You need to do Advanced Math to get into Medicine." I hissed all this at Nick when Mr. Verney was over at Tim Hammer's desk, explaining to Tim again the difference between isosceles and right triangles.

"I thought I made it clear to you last week, I'm not doing Medicine," Nick hissed back.

"This is ridiculous. You topped Advanced Math last year. You shouldn't be here."

"Why? Because it doesn't 'fit' with what everyone wants for my future? You know, I've thought about it and I've come to the conclusion that the only way I'm going to get through to my dad, to you, to everyone, is by making some sort of a statement. So this is it."

Mr. Verney looked up, his mouth in a suspicious curve, told us to get on with our work, then turned back to the triangularly challenged Tim.

So I dropped an eraser on the floor.

"What about the form?" I whispered up to Nick, my face inches from the carpet. "My parents won't sign that form."

"Well then, I'll just have to sign it for them."

*"What?"* My head jolted up, and that's when I hit it on the side of my desk and said, *"Shit!"* louder than was probably appropriate for a Christian school. For Mr. Verney.

That's when Mr. Verney busted us. Told Nick and me that if we had so much to talk about, then we could do it after school. In detention.

I look at my watch. I look at Ms. Michaels, who is sitting at her desk up front marking papers. Fifteen minutes of this detention to go. Fifteen minutes and then I get to have it out with Nick on the bus. Followed by a work shift at the restaurant. I put my head on my arms and wish tomorrow would hurry up.

EIGHTEEN

As soon as Ms. Michaels lets us go, I grab my schoolbag, check I have my work uniform and run to the bus stop. I can't decide whether I should scream abuse at Nick McGowan when he turns up at the bus stop or freeze him out and ignore him. The point is my no-detention record has now been sullied because of him. And there is no way that I'm letting him forge my parents' signatures on a form. He'll get caught for sure. And I'll probably lose my prefects badge.

When I get to Central Avenue, there is only one other student waiting for the later bus. She's carrying a cello. My face clearly communicates the way I feel, because when she recognizes me as a prefect, she pulls two chunky silver rings off her left hand and shoves them in her dress pocket. I turn away. Who cares about her rings? I've got bigger things to think about. My heart is pumping faster than usual. Waiting for Nick to round the corner, I'm feeling revved up and terrified at the same time. Because when he gets here, it's game on.

He turns the corner. Our eyes lock. I glare at him and then turn my back. He walks over to me but I move away. Toward Cello Girl. Things are not quite so easy when the 303 bus arrives. I sit in the old persons' seat at the front and Nick jams himself next to me. He does two kilometers' worth of nagging, all the way to Indooroopilly Shoppingtown.

"What's your father's first name? What does his handwriting look like?"

I stare out the window and ignore him, but he keeps at me.

"You know, you've lived at my house for a week, and this is the most you've ever spoken to me. And it's because you want something. If you think for a second that I'm going to help you in any way forge my parents' signatures—you're delusional."

"Fine."

I go back to staring out the window.

Out of the corner of my eye I watch him unzip his schoolbag, take out his homework diary and start scribbling practice signatures. This is ridiculous.

"My dad's name isn't Eddie, it's Tom. And that signature looks like it was written by someone who's had a stroke. It's appalling. Mr. Jaffers is never going to believe that that is my father's signature."

"Who's Mr. Jaffers?"

"The head of Curriculum and Studies, you idiot."

Then I remember the brochures in my bag. The career brochures that I picked up for Nick McGowan last week. It's now or never. And maybe now is the perfect time.

"Frankly, Nick, I don't think you've thought this through. All this talk about wanting to go back to Middlemount. Okay, so you don't want to be a doctor, but that doesn't mean you're not going to change your mind again. Or you might find another career that still requires you to have done Advanced Math. You know, there are a lot more jobs out there other than just mining and medicine. I was in the Careers Room the other day with Zoë and I found . . ."

I fumble around in my bag, which is on my lap, and produce the fifteen brochures. I know my pitch is sounding dodgy, overly rehearsed, a little wooden. I sound like I'm trying to sell Nick McGowan a set of encyclopedias or something.

"I found some really interesting brochures on different jobs and I was thinking . . ."

"You've *got* to be joking." He glances down at the brochures. "Medical researcher? Dentist?"

"Well . . ."

"Town planner?"

"I just thought—"

"You just thought what? That my life was your business? Well, it's not."

I lean over, grab his schoolbag and start to shove the brochures inside. Nick yanks his schoolbag away from me, but in the process a small blue book falls out. I pick it up. On the front cover in red print it says *The I Hate to Cook Book—More Than 180 Quick and Easy Recipes.* Underneath the title there's a cartoon picture of a rather stunned woman wearing a chef's hat.

"Why on earth have you got a cookbook in your bag?"

Nick snatches the book from me and before I can say anything else is already up and moving to another seat. A seat that's farther down the bus. I look over my shoulder at him, but he's staring out the window with an expression that tells me exactly how he's feeling: pissed off. And as we drive along Moggill Road, I think about how nine days ago Nick McGowan just thought I was uptight; now he hates my guts.

As I turn back around, I notice Cello Girl, her back to me, standing in the open middle section of the bus. I watch her holding on to the back of a seat to keep her balance. She's put her silver rings back on. So I get up, move down the bus, tap her on the shoulder. She turns, and an annoyed expression passes over her face until she sees that it's me. That prefect.

"Nice jewelry," I say. "Consider yourself on detention tomorrow."

I can see in her eyes that she now thinks I'm a bitch. But I don't care. I move back to my seat. It occurs to me that if I'd caught her early this morning, Nick and I would have been on detention with her. Oh God.

When we get to our stop, which also happens to be outside the restaurant where I work, Cello Girl is long gone. I grab my bag and push through some sweaty boys who are playing a handheld video game. But before I'm even off the bus, I see Nick is already walking ahead, up the hill to home.

Fiona Curtis is letting the kids make their own sundaes.

I contemplate this information as I shove my bag into one of the lockers and readjust my red wig in front of the crew-room mirror. Then I turn to Vivian Woo and ask her how she knows. Vivian leans back into the doorway. Ankles crossed, she spins her Brigidine College hat on her finger and says that Susie P. told her. And that Susie was working front counter yesterday when Fiona brought through her birthday-party group and allowed them all—one by one—to make their own sundaes.

Traditionally, this is something that is reserved only for the birthday child. It's a special treat—something to set them apart from their friends. Not anymore, apparently.

I must look shocked. Or pissed off. Or both, because Viv looks at me with sympathy and says, "I know. And apparently she scored really well."

I freeze for a moment, slowly put down my red lipstick and turn to face Vivian.

"I thought scoring wasn't starting until next week?"

"Yeah, I dunno. But they scored her yesterday. I heard

they brought it forward because Simon or Chris is going on holidays."

"What'd she get?"

"Seventeen out of twenty."

"Who scored her?"

"Simon."

We both roll our eyes. I go back to applying my clown mouth. Of course it was Simon, since Fiona has always been one of Simon's favorites.

"What'd she get? How many kids?" I try to ask this nonchalantly, not taking my eyes from the mirror, as though I don't really care what the answer is. The truth is that I care. Boy, do I care. But I can't let Viv know this since—as much as I like her—she's a well-known blab.

"Ten ten-year-olds."

*Ten-year-olds? Talk about easy.* But before I can say anything more than "Pffft," Viv says, "Plus, Fiona is Mrs. Westacott's niece. So as if that's not going to go in her favor."

I turn around—my jaw hanging open in shock. But Viv says she has to go. She just came in to check her roster, and her mum's waiting for her out in the car.

With Vivian gone I think about Fiona Curtis. About the Party Hostess competition. It's a masterstroke, that sundae idea. How could I not have thought of it? I haven't been concentrating, that's why. I've slacked off. It's my own fault. I bite down on my lip and begin to realize now that I had just assumed that I would win this

Party Hostess of the Year competition, hadn't ever seen Fiona Curtis as a serious rival. I just lumped her in with the rest of the hostesses, whose idea of a party is playing a forty-minute game of I Spy. But clearly Fiona Curtis is taking this seriously. She's strategizing at home. She's upping the ante. I'm going to have to pick up my game. And she's related to the owner.

Shit. But I can do this. If I put my mind to this, I can beat her. I have to beat her. And I don't need a gimmick—like Fiona Curtis—to win this thing. Nobody can do a birthday party like me.

I walk into the storeroom and grab the party box. Mrs. Westacott, who owns the Kenmore restaurant with her husband, prepares the boxes at home on the weekends. They're millionaires, apparently. I've never actually seen Mrs. Westacott, but in my head she looks like Mrs. Howell from *Gilligan's Island*. I've always imagined her as a haughty woman with a poodle face, wearing a fur coat and pearls, who sits at a dining table and prepares our weekly birthday-party boxes. I figure she'd be the type of person who says *"Dah-ling"* a lot. My eyes skim the contents of the box and see the usual balloons, birthday-cake candles, party bags. I peel my party profile off the side of the box. Six kids. Five-year-old girls. Birthday girl's name is Sally. My confidence rises. Five-year-olds love me. Let's just see Fiona Curtis try and beat me at this. Nepotism be damned, I'm going to win this. I head off into the restaurant thinking, *Party Hostess of the Year? Piece of cake.*

NINETEEN

Piece of shit cake, more like it.

At first, everything goes like clockwork. We play Simon Says, we do some coloring, we tour the restaurant. Chris, the manager on duty, is standing in the corner with a clipboard and a pen. He even gives me two thumbs-up—that's how well it's going. Until I send the kids out into the restaurant playground. A playground that usually only features monkey bars. Swings. A slide. But today what I don't know is that it also features a poo. Monkey bars, swings, a slide and a poo. One minute I'm sending Sally and her friends outside to play. The next minute the little girls are tearing back inside. Screaming. Screaming about poo.

"*There's a poo!*" they scream hysterically, over and over, waving their little arms in the air like Muppets on speed.

A quick investigation reveals that Sally's three-year-old little brother has crept into the playground, pulled down his pants and done an enormous shit on the Astroturf. On the bright side—if there can be a bright side to poos in playgrounds—the poo looks easy to clean up. Sort of. On the not-so-bright side he did it at the bottom of the slide. A slide that just minutes ago Sally and two of her friends slid down headfirst. Headfirst into turdsville.

I try to stay calm amid the hysteria. I look around at the little girls. Screaming and crying seem reasonable when some of their heads have passed through the poo of a three-year-old. There's poo in hair. On braids. In hair ribbons. The other three just seem mildly traumatized by the afternoon's events. I look at Sally's mum, who is saying, "This has got to stop" in a rather fierce voice to Sally's smug-looking little brother. Then I look at Chris, who is pacing back and forth and talking into a headset. When he eventually starts writing on the clipboard again, he's shaking his head in a way that tells me that poo has no part in this restaurant's mission statement. And that I'm being marked down. *This is an act of God,* I want to say. *It shouldn't count against my score. That poo was beyond my control.* But nobody's listening. Chris motions for me to come over. In a weary tone he says that I should keep going with the party "as best I can" and that he's organized for another crew member to help me clean up. As I usher the five-year-olds into the toilets, Fiona Curtis rounds the corner with a mop and bucket.

TWENTY

I'm in the mother of all bad moods when I get home. I've literally had a shit day. I've been given my first-ever detention. Nick McGowan is finally talking to me again, but only because he wants me to sign some stupid form. There was the whole poo thing at work. Worse, Fiona Curtis was unspeakably friendly to me as she mopped poo on the Astroturf. I'm tired. And grumpy. And fed up with everybody and everything. And to top it all off, as soon as I walk into the kitchen I see that Mum has cooked apricot chicken for dinner. I *hate* apricot chicken. Fruit and poultry have no place together.

During the meal itself there's an added level of tension. Nick and I sit in frosty silence with the haunted look of hostages. Not that my parents seem to notice—they're too busy discussing Caitlin's latest financial dilemma in Paris and remain oblivious to the cold war being waged around them. My mood is not helped when my mother finally turns her attention to me and orders me to stop slouching. She then tells me that my bangs need a cut and offers to cut them for me after dinner. I remind her that the last time I let her cut my hair, she gave me "economy bangs." They were so short that I looked like a chipmunk. She rolls her eyes as though I am exaggerating. I remind her that even Dad started calling me Alvin. She says, "Well, just push them out of your eyes" and then leans over and does it for me, brutally pushing my bangs and a fair amount of my skin across my forehead. I respond by saying, "Ow!" even though it doesn't hurt.

And then, in what can only be considered a blatant move to antagonize me, Nick McGowan for the second time offers to do the washing-up. Knowing that my parents will make me do it with him. Knowing that this is completely throwing my study timetable out of whack. And my parents, rather than insisting that as a guest he do no chores, revel in it. My mother, in particular, seems to be enjoying this new world order. Her response to my protests is to pour herself a sherry and say, "It'll take you no time at all, Rach. Nick's helping you."

So I reluctantly get up from the table, start clearing the plates and contemplate the effectiveness of stabbing myself to death with a butter knife.

"I cannot *belieeeve* you've done this again." I start to scrub burned apricot chicken from the casserole dish.

He nods. It is the nod of someone who couldn't care less.

"Aren't you going to say anything?"

"You missed a bit."

I turn and glare at Nick McGowan, who is pointing with a deadpan expression to some cheese still on a fork.

"Fine." I snatch the fork back from him and scrub it so hard I half expect the prongs to snap.

"There." I thrust it back at him. "You're pathetic, by the way."

"Really?"

"Yes."

"Well, I'd rather be pathetic than what you are."

"Which is?"

"Spoiled. I've watched you for a week, and your mum does everything for you. You don't even appreciate it."

I turn and stare at him. "No she doesn't."

He rolls his eyes and says, "Yeah, right. She makes your lunch every day. Does all your washing and ironing. Cooks your dinner. She's like that butler on TV—Benson."

"Yeah? And you're like the poster boy for Benson & Hedges. At least I'm doing something with my spare time. Like *studying*. All you seem to do is suck up to my parents, eat our food, smoke cigarettes and play crap music way too loud. Last night I could barely concentrate on my English because you were playing some absolute crap music so loud it was coming through the floorboards."

He looks up at me with a combined look of horror and disdain. "I was playing the Ramones."

"Whatever. We have exams in a few weeks. Exams that count toward our final grade. I mean, your parents—"

"Par*ent*. Single. My mum died. So it's just me and my dad."

I stare back at Nick, unsure how to continue.

"When I was two. She died when I was two. So your point is?"

"Well . . ." I struggle to remember the point I was trying to make. "Well, your dad would be paying a fortune for you to be at this school, and your biggest concern is whether or not I do the washing-up."

"Trust me, I have bigger concerns in my life than—"

"Oh, that's right. Like forging my parents' signatures. Just in case I didn't make myself 100 percent clear on the bus this afternoon, I'm not helping you. I'm not helping you drop down into my Math class."

The phone starts to ring. Elbow-deep in suds, I holler, "Can somebody get that, please?"

"Coming, coming." Dad appears round the corner and grabs the phone. "It's probably your sister."

"Asking for more money for the third time in a week."

"Just one moment," says my father to the caller. Then he turns around and says, "Nick, it's Sam Wilks for you."

I look at Nick. But unlike last time, his face doesn't go pale. Instead, he just turns to my dad and says in a guarded tone, "Would you mind if I took it downstairs?"

Mum walks in, picks up the tea towel and takes over the drying. As I pass her the plates, we talk about my upcoming English assignment. About what we're doing in French. About Zoë's latest run-in with Mrs. Finemore. And through it all she laughs and says, "You girls," the way she does when she catches Caitlin and me plotting some ridiculous scheme. When the last plate has been dried and put away, she says, "Darling, will you bring Gipper in from the veranda for me?"

"Sure." I head out to the veranda to fetch our ten-year-old canary.

"You know, Nick helped me prepare tonight's dinner. And this afternoon he completely cleaned out Gipper's cage for me."

"Fabulous," I say. *Brownnoser*, I think.

I look out to the backyard. I spot Nick's outline down by the pool. He's out there now, resting his head in his hands, his phone call long finished. I stand there and wonder what is really going on in Nick McGowan's life. I think about his decision to drop down to Math in Society and wonder if I'm doing the right thing by refusing to help him forge Mum's and Dad's signatures on the consent form. I look up at the stars and say, "Please don't let the rest of the year be like today."

I turn around to Gipper and grab the cage handle.

"Come on, Gip. Time for you to go to bed."

When I look down into the cage, I see bright blue paper with the words TOWN PLANNER and DENTIST and PSYCHIATRIST—all sprinkled with bird poo and feathers and husks. He's lined the floor of Gipper's cage with the career brochures I gave him.

TWENTY-ONE

I venture out of my bedroom at eight o'clock to give myself a five-minute break before I start on Biology. I bump into Mum in the hallway.

"I'm about to dish up some ice cream. Do you want some?"

"Nah."

"Well, do me a favor—"

"And ask Nick?"

She nods.

I roll my eyes.

"And remind him"—she hands me the cordless phone—"that it's Tuesday, and he's supposed to call his dad."

It's a while before he notices me standing there, in the shadows, watching him smoke. When he finally turns and sees me, he seems neither surprised nor annoyed by my presence. Instead, he just taps his cigarette into the mug, off-loads some ash and says, "You again" before turning back to look at the moon.

"Benson wants to know if you want some ice cream."

Nick McGowan turns his head and looks at me. His eyes narrow, but his lips form a wry smile. He's looking at me differently now, as though I've surprised him by making a joke.

"No thanks."

An awkward silence descends.

"Mum said to remind you to call your dad."

I hold the phone out to him. He stares at it as though what I'm offering him is a gun. So I lay the phone down on the box beside him and turn to leave, in a sudden hurry to get away.

"I do all the cooking at home."

I stop. Turn back around.

"That's why I had a recipe book in my bag. I'm on a mission to find a good lasagna recipe."

I don't know what to say. So I just sort of stare at Nick McGowan.

"It's all about the béchamel sauce. And the layering," he says, nodding, not even looking at me. "Yep."

"Right," I say.

"My dad likes lasagna," he says, picking up the cord-less phone and bouncing it up and down in his hand. "So at least I'll have something to say to my dad tonight.

I can say, 'Hey, Dad, got another lasagna recipe for us to try.'"

His tone is sarcastic.

I start to make a move to leave.

"Rachel?"

"Yeah?" I turn and look him in the eye.

"I just want you to know, I think your parents are great—you don't know how good you've got it."

# TWENTY-TWO

I leave for school extra early the next morning so that I can avoid seeing Nick McGowan. Yet all day at school, without me wanting them to, my eyes search for him. Scanning classrooms, skirting over people's heads down long corridors, jumping from person to person in the quadrangle, by the tennis courts, in the library, in the cafeteria line. I never see him. In English, when we're supposed to be watching the second half of *Hamlet,* I find myself staring out the window, wishing he would pass by. I imagine that Nick McGowan and I are like two characters in one of those old sixties movies starring Doris Day and Rock Hudson, hunting for each other and missing each other by seconds. As I leave a room, he enters it and vice versa. Then eventually we'd back into each other in the library among the shelves. Books would fall, and we'd laugh and make up.

I allow myself to imagine this scenario right up until Mrs. Ramsay taps me on the shoulder outside my English classroom and asks if Nick McGowan is home sick today. I feel sick.

"Well, I left home early this morning because I was on gate duty, so . . ." *Please drop this. Please drop this.*

"How is he?"

"Um, well . . ."

"I think those phone calls he's been receiving from Sam have come as a bit of a shock." She flips open her appointment book and taps the page. "He was supposed to come and see me today at morning tea to talk about it all again—how he was feeling about the calls—but just tell him to come to my office at morning tea tomorrow. It's important that he continue to talk this all through with me."

I say, "Okay." But what I really want to say is, *What the hell is going on?*

Something in my face must give me away. Mrs. Ramsay is bending down now, trying to look into my eyes, touching my forearm.

"Is everything okay, Rachel? How are you finding it all with Nick moving in?"

Oh God, she's trying to do a hit-and-run counseling session on me. Outside my English classroom. With people walking past.

"I'm fine. Everything is okay."

"Just okay?"

"Good. It's good having Nick here." I look around as I say this, hoping no one is noticing that I'm talking to the school counselor.

"So"—her eyes narrow—"is Nick at home sick today? I know it's a half day for you seniors, but he still can't afford to start missing class."

This is my chance, I realize. To tell her about the Math in Society consent form, about the smoking and the phone calls, about the fact that I am fairly sure Nick McGowan is skipping school today. And it's the right thing to do. It's what I should do.

"I think Nick may have woken up with a migraine or something. I left early, so I'm not sure."

Her brow furrows.

"Pretty sure. I'm pretty sure."

Her face immediately relaxes.

"Oh." She straightens back up. "Oh, well, that's all right then. Well, just tell him to come and see me tomorrow and we'll schedule in a new appointment time."

I pick some imaginary lint off my dress and say, "Absolutely."

TWENTY-THREE

"Hello?" I walk out of the kitchen and into the lounge. "Anyone home?"

It's one-thirty p.m. and the house is completely empty.

I kick off my school shoes and pad barefoot into the kitchen, on the hunt for some food. There's a jar of almond bread on the kitchen counter, with a note from my mother taped to the lid. I pull it off. She wants me to bring the washing in off the line. I sigh. The fact that I'm in Year 12 and have an extraordinary amount of work to do seems to be lost on everyone these days. I grab three pieces of almond bread and wonder where Nick McGowan is right now. Wonder what he's doing. And that's when I spot him. Through the kitchen window. Barefoot, in his gray school shorts, with his blue-and-maroon school shirt unbuttoned and hanging out, Nick McGowan is cleaning our pool. I watch him deftly maneuver the long metallic pole of the scoop through the water, like some kind of Venetian gondolier.

"What are you doing?"

He looks up over the top of his sunglasses and sees me standing now at the top of the steps, which lead down to the pool. I notice that his blond curls look almost white in the summer heat.

"The pool was dirty."

"So?"

"So I decided to clean it."

"Where were you today?"

"At school."

"No you weren't."

"Okay, Rachel, so I wasn't. Big deal." He goes back to concentrating on netting more leaves and twigs from the water's surface, not looking at me when he speaks. "I was out enjoying this beautiful, sunny day while you and everyone else"—he pauses as he lifts the scoop out of the water, shakes the captured leaves and twigs onto the grass and then returns the net to the water—"were stuck indoors at desks learning stuff that you'll most likely never use again. You'll never get this day back. It's another day you've wasted."

"I've wasted? You're on drugs. So is this what you're gonna do now? Tiptoe through the tulips instead of going to school?"

He pauses and looks into the distance. "Maybe."

I make a snorting sound in disgust.

"Why do you even care?" He looks directly at me, eyebrows raised.

"I don't. I don't care what you do. What I care about is when Mrs. Ramsay comes and finds me to ask where you are. 'Is Nick home sick today, Rachel? It's just that he hasn't shown up to any of his classes.'"

"Aah." He continues to skim the water's surface with the pool scoop, taking a few small steps to the left as he negotiates the far back corner.

"Yes, aah. Apparently, idiot head, you had an appointment to see her today. If you're going to start skipping class, try not to make it on days when the school counselor is expecting to see you in her office."

I turn to walk back up to the house.

He calls out, "What did you tell her?"

But I keep walking.

TWENTY-FOUR

I don't feel like dinner, so I spend the evening sitting on the floor of my bedroom just staring at my copy of *Hamlet*. Part of our assignment is to memorize a three-to-five-minute soliloquy and perform it in front of the rest of the class. Ms. Corelli's giving us two weeks to get it done, but I want to get a start on it now. I don't like leaving things to the last minute. I stare down at the words from one of Ophelia's monologues. I don't even understand what half of these words mean. According to my CliffsNotes, Ophelia's telling her father, Polonius, that she thinks Hamlet has gone mad. But Hamlet is only pretending to be mad because he suspects his uncle killed his father to be with Hamlet's mother and therefore become king. Talk about dysfunctional.

I close my eyes and attempt to recite the first verse for the hundredth time.

> *My lord, as I was sewing in my chamber,*
> *Lord Hamlet,—with his doublet all unbrac'd;*
> *No hat upon his head; his stockings foul'd,*
> *Ungart'red, and down-gyved to his ankle;*
> *Pale as his shirt; his knees knocking each other;*

I open my eyes and take a quick peek at the book. *That's right—the double-*p *line.*

> *And with a look so piteous in purport*
> *As if he had been loosed out of hell*
> *To speak of horrors,—he comes before me.*

Why is it that I have been able to memorize all the words to Billy Joel's "We Didn't Start the Fire" but I can't even get eight lines from *Hamlet* down? And I've got another dozen or so to go. This is Nick McGowan's fault. I can't concentrate. My mind keeps wandering away from Hamlet and his unbraced doublet and over to Nick McGowan. He's really not even that good-looking. I mean, okay, so he has really big green eyes that are, like, I don't know, the color of sea glass or something. But he has a slightly crooked nose. And his eyes, I'm pretty sure, are too far apart.

I look down at my books. I repeat the "piteous in

purport" line a few more times, but I keep saying "pitiful" instead of "piteous." I toss *Hamlet* aside and look around my room. I notice my purse lying open on the floor. That's what I'll do, I'll reorganize my purse. Then I'll make a fresh start on the monologue. Using my foot, I nudge my purse to within arm's reach. Then I immediately pull everything out of it. For some reason cleaning out my purse always makes me feel better. What I don't expect to discover halfway through my ritual is that my library card is missing. I pull everything out of my purse all over again. Perhaps it is stuck to another card, like my Video Ezy card? It's not stuck to my Video Ezy card. I pull everything out of my schoolbag (which includes six textbooks, a plastic container of dried apricots, three school newsletters, a weepy red pen, two old crumpled bus tickets and a hair band). I check the pockets of my dress, my pencil case, Dad's car. I search my schoolbag again. This is unlike me. Caitlin loses things. Zoë loses things. I'm organized. I have places and systems. I don't *lose* things.

Except, apparently, my library card. Shit.

I sit on the floor and contemplate the hassle of having to report my library card as lost and arrange for a new one. Where did I have it last? Where did I have it last?

The bedside table.

I left my library card in the bedside-table drawer next to the bed downstairs. In Nick's room.

He watches me walk down the courtyard steps to the pool area, and as I march toward him he calls out, "How now, Ophelia?"

My brow furrows in response.

"Your window's open." His eyes flicker up to my room. "It's been a bit like Shakespeare in the Park down here. If I didn't know how much you hated my guts, I'd think you were serenading me."

"In your dreams."

"So do you like it?"

"What?"

"Shakespeare. *Hamlet.*"

I shrug.

"I like *him*. Hamlet. I like him the best out of all of Shakespeare's protagonists," he announces, with more conviction than I expect.

"How come?" I ask, trying to remember what "protagonist" means.

"Well . . ." He searches my face as though he suspects the answer is written in faint pen on my forehead. Then he says, "Miss Kennedy explained that Hamlet's feeling a certain amount of guilt and doesn't know how to cope with it. So really it's about him struggling with making the right decision. He's complex and flawed and . . ."

"And a wimp. And a procrastinator who sits around all day complaining about his life but never doing anything about it. And you're going to get lung cancer if you don't stop smoking."

With that he takes a long drag and then exhales the smoke, blowing it this time into one big billowy circle.

"What are you doing?"

"I'm offering you a friendship ring."

"I'm not signing the form, Nick."

"I know." I can tell from his tone that he's not going to hassle me about it anymore.

I don't know what else to say, so I turn to leave.

"So was Mrs. Ramsay suspicious?"

I turn back around.

"No. Because I covered for you."

He nods slowly. "Where did you say I was?"

"I said you were at home with a migraine, okay?" But I don't wait to hear his reaction because I'm not interested. I just walk straight back up to the house.

It's not until I'm walking back up the courtyard steps that I realize I never asked him if I could go into his room to fetch my library card. I stand outside his bedroom door. I look out the window and see him hugging his knees and staring up at the sky. I look back at his bedroom door. I'm going in.

I push the door open and tentatively take a few steps inside. Looking around, I feel a little disappointed. His room is not so different from the way I left it the Sunday he moved in. There are no posters on the wall, no photo frames adorning the desk. Just yesterday's school uniform lying in a heap on the floor. His schoolbag is dumped in the middle of the room, and I can see one of his German books sitting on top. It's disappointing. There's nothing much to see. I walk over to the bedside table and pull open the drawer to get my library card. I'm not sure why, but I'm a little surprised when I see stuff—his stuff—in there. A watch. Some loose change. A small red plastic photo album. My library card is sitting in the far back corner. I immediately grab it and push it into my pocket and go to shut the drawer.

Except I don't. I sit on the edge of his bed, slide the drawer back open and stare at the contents the way I used to stare into my mum's jewelry box when I was little. My fingers stroke the plastic cover of the photo album. I pick it up. There's only half a dozen photos in it. The first pic is a photo of a cattle dog. This must be Frank. The photo is a close-up. Taken of Frank as he's straining to lick the camera. Then there are a couple of photos of Nick and another guy—some mate from Middlemount. In one shot they're sitting on the back of a truck squinty-eyed and grinning. The friend is wearing a beaten-up cowboy hat. Nick looks different—more country or something. I stare at the photo and think about what Nick said to his dad on the phone that first night. About wanting to go back to Middlemount, back to his real life.

In the next photo Nick and this boy are dressed in football jerseys. His friend has him in a playful headlock. What is it with guys and headlocks? And farting, for that matter. I keep flipping. There are two photos of Nick with a man who has to be his father. They have the same mouth. His father has kind eyes. And a big belly hanging over his jeans. And there's a photo of a young woman with long blond hair cradling a baby in her arms. This must be Nick's mother. She's beautiful.

But that's it for photos. There aren't any more. I put the album back. I slide the drawer closed. Bounce up and down on the bed gently. Look around the room. I turn behind me and lift up his pillow. There's a pair of blue Garfield boxer shorts there. I drop the pillow back down. Then I notice I have my left foot on a booklet of some sort on the floor. I pick it up. On the cover in big blue letters it says *Feeling Blue: The Facts on Depression*. I stare at the cover and then notice some brochures sticking out from inside the booklet. I pull them out. One's a brochure on handling grief. The other is on suicide prevention.

TWENTY-FIVE

I can't sleep. I lie awake blinking into the dark. I keep thinking about the brochures. That booklet. Part of me feels really, really bad about snooping. The other part of me wants to understand why Nick McGowan has brochures on depression and suicide in his room. I start to wonder again what happened to him over the summer, wonder if the rumors are true that he actually tried to kill himself. I try to picture Nick going into a shed and taking an overdose of anything. Frankly, I just can't picture it.

I start to think about suicide. I remember the time Rhonda Daniels told a group of us in the dayroom that if you want to slit your wrists, you have to slice up the arm, not across like everyone thinks. Even in *Hamlet,* Ophelia drowns herself in the river because she finds out

Hamlet doesn't love her and that her father has been murdered. I think about drowning. The thought of it just makes me shudder—not being able to breathe. I used to hate it when my uncle Dave would hold my head under the water in the pool as a joke. If I was going to kill myself, that's not the way I'd do it. Not that I sit around thinking about killing myself. Although there was one time when I thought about it briefly. It was when I was really stressed about my grades last year in Year 11. It wasn't a great year for me. In Year 10 I'd been able to get high grades without really having to do any work. I sailed through. I loved Year 10. But that all changed in Year 11. Everything was harder. Teachers kept talking about grades and final results. Despite having achieved distinctions in the Westpac math competition in Years 9 and 10, now I couldn't keep up with Advanced Math. Things were just more difficult. To make things worse, my skin was psychotic and my face was constantly red and blotchy.

There was this one week in particular when everything was really shitty. I put a huge amount of work into a Biology assignment and got a really bad mark. In English, Leo Bremmer dropped a pencil on the floor and looked up my dress. He told all the other boys that I was wearing pink undies. And that I had fat legs. And at the same time Mum and Dad were on my back about everything. I remember one night just sitting in my room crying. We had swimming the next day, and I was going to have to be in a bathing suit in front of Leo and the other boys. All I could think about was that I didn't want them to see me. See my legs. And then after a while I'd cried so much that I was numb, and for a few seconds I thought about what it would be like to end it all. Fade to black. Kill myself. To not have to be here to deal with this.

But it was a thought that came and went pretty quickly. For starters, if I killed myself it would bloody hurt. Plus, I'd never get to see what happened between Bronny and Henry on *Neighbours*. I remember mentioning it to Zee the next day at morning tea, and she heavily advised against it. She said she'd miss me, for one thing. She'd thought about suicide once, too, she said. When her parents split up on the first day of Expo last year. But she realized she was too lazy to even kill herself. Who could be bothered? She also pointed out that knowing our luck, we'd kill ourselves the day before we got a prize for something. Or just days before we were destined to meet our soul mates. Or won the trip to New York in a contest that we'd both entered in *Cleo* magazine. She was right. Not that either of us won the New York trip, but I did win ten dollars on a scratch ticket later that week. And she kissed someone at a Melissa Etheridge concert. As for swimming, I wore a pair of maroon board shorts over my swimsuit and nobody said a thing. A week later another five girls followed suit.

I wonder if Nick McGowan is thinking that this is as good as it gets for him. That there are no great moments round the corner waiting to happen. No New York trips.

No ten-dollar scratch tickets. No rock-concert kisses. No board-shorts solutions. Just a long, lonely highway of being pushed into doing something that he feels he can't deliver.

And a girl who won't sign a form. A girl he lives with who won't help him.

TWENTY-SIX

Thursday morning Dad offers to give Nick and me an early lift to school since he has to be in the office for a conference call and I'm still on gate duty for the rest of the week.

I sit in the front passenger seat. Nick sits behind me. I can't look at him. I feel like I know too much and that he'll know, just by looking at me, that I was snooping in his room last night. So as soon as Dad starts the car, I immediately reach for the radio and turn it on. No matter how much Caitlin and I beg, Dad won't let us listen to FM104. It's the ABC all the way with my father. So we spend the twenty-minute drive to school listening to callers phone in complaining about the cost of buses. The rubbish bin collection schedule. Our lord mayor's hairstyle. For once I'm just grateful that there is something to fill the silence.

Getting our bags out of the trunk, Nick and I don't speak. Then I stand on the footpath and watch Dad's car do a U-turn. As usual, I make sure that I wave goodbye as he heads off to the city. Then he's gone and it's just me and Nick. I walk ahead and keep thinking that I need to break the silence. As I walk through the gates, I hear myself saying, "Are you catching the bus this afternoon?"

When I get no reply, I turn around to hear Nick's response, only to see his back. He's walking down the road in the opposite direction, toward the train station.

"Hey!"

He doesn't turn around. Just keeps walking.

*"Nick!"*

I throw my schoolbag behind a tree and chase after him. Which means that I'm panting by the time I reach him.

"Where are you going?"

"Dunno. Today I thought I might catch a movie over there." He points to the Eldorado Cinema across from the train station.

"I'll sign the form."

"What?"

"If you come back to school with me, I'll sign it. I'll sign it now."

TWENTY-SEVEN

I'm preoccupied all morning because of that form. Knowing that Math in Society is period 3. Knowing that Nick McGowan is going to hand in that form to Mr. Verney. In French Mrs. Lesage talks about our first-term French exam—and instead of listening and taking notes, I sit there and keep writing my mum's signature over and over in the back of my French book. Is the *P* too big? I suddenly can't remember how Mum does her *r*'s. Will the "Patricia Hill" scribbled on that change-of-subject consent form look fake? Will Mr. Verney cross-check it against some other form my mother has signed in the past?

My stomach twists and pulls and I feel decidedly unwell. I'm tempted to pack up my things and go back to Rocking Horse Records—swear some more at the sales assistant, offend some more nanas.

An adult hand appears from behind me and flips my *Action* French book to the appropriate page. I look up. Mrs. Lesage raises her eyebrows at me.

*"Pardonnez-moi, madame,"* I mumble.

She keeps walking to the blackboard and starts yakking on about a talk we have to give—in French—about a famous French person.

I look down at my French book, at the practiced signature, and suddenly remember that Mum always writes her *r*'s with a small loop on the left. I didn't do it that way.

A little voice inside my head whispers, *There's a train to the city at seven past ten.*

Okay. So as soon as this class is over, I'm going to head for the station. I've done it before. Who's gonna stop me?

The bell goes.

The class immediately stands up, but Mrs. Lesage says, *"Asseyez-vous, s'il vous plaît"* and makes us all sit back down and copy down our homework for tomorrow.

When she says, *"Vous êtes libres pour aller,"* it's like she's waved a checkered flag at a speedway. Students rush for the door like the desks are on fire. Except me. Today my legs are like lead. With each step toward the Math classroom I tell myself that it would be okay for me to get the train, how high my chances of getting away with it would be. Even when I'm standing outside the Math classroom, watching my classmates go inside, a voice in my head keeps saying, *Go now. It's not too late.*

Then Mr. Verney and his Road Runner tie round the corner. "Inside, please," he says to me and to Janine Poulous, who's in the middle of a Deep and Meaningful with her boyfriend, some Year 11 guy.

I go inside. Take a seat. The way I always knew I would. But Nick's not here.

Mr. Verney shuts the door. "All right, folks, show me the homework you did from yesterday."

He's changed his mind. Realized that swapping over to Math in Society is not the answer.

The knots in my stomach begin to loosen just as Nick McGowan races through the door like someone breaking in to save hostages. He looks around, runs his fingers through his hair and, suddenly self-conscious, jams the piece of paper he's holding into his mouth while he uses both hands to tuck in his disheveled shirt.

Mr. Verney looks pointedly at his watch and says, "Aah, Mr. McGowan, how nice of you to join us."

"Sorry, I was with Mrs. Ramsay. She told me to give you this." Nick hands over to Mr. Verney the note that now doubles as a dental record.

Mr. Verney purses his lips in a skeptical fashion. Reads it. Nods.

"And I have that signed consent form," says Nick, reaching into his back pocket.

"You're just full of forms today, aren't you, Mr. McGowan?"

Nick hands him the form, smiles weakly and says, "Yes, sir." Meanwhile, I resist the urge to vomit as I watch Mr. Verney's eyes scan down for the requisite signatures. Nick doesn't even look nervous.

"Very well. Welcome to the magic and the mystery that is Math in Society. You can have this textbook until you get your own." Mr. Verney hands Nick his copy of *Let's Learn Math!* by D. M. Barry (who thinks that adding an exclamation mark to a title makes Venn diagrams and prime numbers more exciting—go figure).

Book in hand, Nick turns now to face the class, looking for a seat. Our eyes meet. Nick mouths, *Relax!* His eyes are amused, full of daring, telling me that we've gotten away with it, as though we're the new Bonnie and Clyde. Then he winks at me.

Mr. Verney lets out an impatient sigh. "Do hurry up and take a seat, Mr. McGowan."

"Sorry." Nick makes a face at me as though Mr. Verney is quietly mad. I can't help but smile back.

Then he takes the spare seat next to Sarah Neele and the lesson—the idiot's guide to trigonometry—begins. And I realize we've gotten away with it.

TWENTY-EIGHT

Zoë spends our entire lunch hour trying to convince me to come up to Indooroopilly Shoppingtown after school. She has to work in her mother's shop from four until six p.m. and reckons she'll die without any visitors. I haven't told Zoë about the brochures I found in Nick's room or about the consent form I signed for him. I'm not sure why—although I suspect that it's easier telling other people's secrets than your own. Plus, if I talk about it out loud, it'll seem even more real—and wrong. And at the moment I'm convincing myself that it'll all work out okay: Nick will eventually tell his dad that he's dropped down to Math in Society, Mr. McGowan will accept it and my parents will never find out. I'm not ready for Zoë's honesty. Sometimes it stings like alcohol on a cut.

When I walk into CopperWorld, Zoë's serving a customer, so I take the opportunity to look around. It's a strange shop. Zoë's mum has owned it for as long as I can remember. It's a shop that seems to specialize in gold-painted potted-plant holders, plastic flowers, touch lamps and fake mahogany full-length mirrors—"in crap," as Zoë likes to say. Zoë reckons this shop sucks the life right out of her. She spends most of her days accidentally chipping the furniture when she vacuums and then coloring the scratches in with a black Nikko pen.

Finally, Zoë's at the register, ringing up a wooden hat stand. It's another few minutes before the customer has left the shop.

"Hey," she says, walking over to me while simultaneously opening out a plastic fern. I can tell by the look on her face that she's worried about something.

"What's up? What's wrong?"

She sighs dramatically.

"Nothing."

"Zoë!"

"Well . . ."

"Well . . ."

"Well, I just asked the Psychic Lettuce what my future holds, and it said, 'You will live alone with sixty guinea pigs. And they will all be called Peter.'"

"Hang on a second. You asked what? Did you say *Psychic Lettuce*?"

She puts the fern down.

"It's a lettuce that predicts your future. I found it at the games arcade next door."

"Lettuce as in vegetable? As in iceberg and romaine? There's a lettuce in this shopping center claiming to have psychic abilities?"

"Yes."

"Where?"

Zoë grabs my hand and leads me out the door—but not before flipping the BACK IN FIVE MINUTES sign on the shop door and locking the door behind her. She proceeds to drag me to the games arcade. In between the motorbike game and Space Invaders is a black machine with PSYCHIC LETTUCE written on the front. Stepping up to the machine, I see that a cartoon lettuce complete with googly eyes and a mouth—a lettuce that frankly looks like a drug addict—is offering to tell me my future.

"Do it!" Zoë pushes me in the arm. "Do it!"

"All right." I rub my arm defensively. "What do I have to do?"

"Put in forty cents, and then when it says, 'Tell me my future, Lettuce,' you hit the big red button."

I put in my forty cents. I click the big red button: The lettuce's eyes begin to whirl. Within seconds, up pops the following message: "You will discover a new use for empty milk cartons and be the first self-made billionaire under twenty."

"*Ohmygod!* How lucky are you?"

"Zoë, I am not going to discover a new use for

milk cartons, believe me. And as for your prediction, you are not going to end up alone living with sixty guinea pigs. . . ."

"Who are all named Peter."

"Right. You hate animals. And even if you *did* have sixty guinea pigs, as if you'd call them all Peter."

"Yeah. I hate that name."

"Exactly. And you're gorgeous. Do not listen to an allegedly clairvoyant vegetable. Okay?"

And as I say that, Zoë pushes in another forty cents and smacks the red button again. "Your grandmother will leave you a great big house . . . that's haunted!" says the lettuce (who I suspect is doing tequila shots in between readings because its eyes are becoming more bloodshot).

*"Ohmygod!"* Zoë pushes me over. "A haunted house!"

"Zoë! *Zoë!*" I snap my fingers in front of her face. "That lettuce is on drugs. Think about it. Your gran lives in an apartment in Toowong. This is a stupid game developed by some stupid guy in America who is trying to suck money out of people. It's *not real.*"

"You're right." We begin to walk out of the arcade and back to CopperWorld. "And the Psychic Lettuce isn't half as accurate as *The Destiny Book.*"

I bite my tongue.

Zoë goes behind the counter of CopperWorld. I follow her.

"Here," she says, thrusting a hardcover black book

toward me. "Mum bought it for Megan's birthday last week. Think of a question and then open it up at any page."

"All right." Against my better judgment I close my eyes. What I should be asking is, *Will Nick and I get away with the forged Math form?* But the question that keeps coming into my head is, *What does Nick McGowan think of me?* I flip open the book.

"What does it say?"

"It says, 'Probably tomorrow.'" I try to keep the disappointment out of my voice. Stupid book.

"What did you ask?"

I lie and say, "I asked, 'Will Zoë shut up soon?'"

"*Ohmygod!* That is *très* spooky!"

And just when I am about to prove *The Destiny Book* wrong by throwing it at Zoë's head and rendering her temporarily unconscious, the bell above the shop door jingles.

"I just wanted to inquire about the sign on the window. The position vacant?"

We both turn and see a young woman standing at the counter.

"What star sign are you?" asks Zoë, in a tone that makes her sound like a poor man's Nancy Drew.

"Oh, um, Cancer?" she says, as though she's not quite sure.

"Oh dear, well, no . . . *obviously.* But thanks."

The girl looks confused. "Oh, right, okay." She wanders back out the door.

I look at Zoë, eyebrows raised.

"What?"

"What did you say that for?"

"She wasn't aesthetically pleasing."

"What? You can't just dismiss someone based on their looks. You know, she might have been great. She might have had heaps of retail experience."

"Riiight. But you can't possibly expect me to spend all day looking at that face. She looked like the pope. It was creepy."

"She did *not* look like the pope."

"The pope with a perm."

"She did not look like the pope with a perm."

"And she had dry and unmanageable hair."

"What's her hair got to do with it? You know, I think maybe you need to sit down and really think about the type of person your mum wants to employ. What qualities they need to have. *Retail experience,* you know."

"You're so blah." She rolls her eyes.

"Don't roll your eyes at me."

"Hello? Cranky Island, population: you. Anyway, before you got here I asked the Psychic Lettuce if you're supposed to come to the cast party tomorrow night."

I roll my eyes. "For the hundredth time, I'm *not* going."

Zoë raises her eyebrows, crosses her arms and looks up at the ceiling.

"Fine. What did the Great Lettuce say?"

She gives a smug little smile and says, "It said, 'Yes, absolutely.'"

TWENTY-NINE

I can't believe I'm listening to a lettuce.

This is how sad my life has become. A lettuce has become my social-life consultant. Next I'll be conferring with carrots about my hairstyle.

I look in the mirror at what I'm wearing. No matter how hard I try, I never seem to look right. Kate Winter always looks perfect. Immaculate. Every month when we have a dress-down day at school, she walks through the gates as though she's just come straight from a Country Road catalog shoot. I never do. Sometimes I've even gone so far as to buy the exact same outfit that appears on the store mannequins in Cherry Lane, and it still doesn't look the same on me. Even my clothing seems disappointed.

"What are you doing up there? Hurry up!" Zoë's voice fires through the house like a gunshot.

"Keep your pants on! I'm coming!" I scream back with alarming alacrity.

I adjust the shoulder pads in my green-and-white-striped top and fix the big, thick black belt that hangs over it and my stonewashed jeans. I *so-o-o* don't want to go to this tonight. Still, how bad can it be? And at least they're not holding it at Café 104 like they did last year.

I fling open my bedroom door and say, "I'm only staying for an hour, so—"

Standing next to Zoë is Nick McGowan. He's dressed as if he's coming. With us.

I walk down the stairs to where they're standing, keeping my eyes on Nick McGowan. He smiles. But all I can think of to say is, "Are you coming?"

"Yep."

"Technically, he was stage crew last year," says Zoë.

"I don't remember you—"

"Mr. Jacobs got Nick and Stuart Zucker to run the coatroom during the first performance."

"I hope you all aren't turning up empty-handed. I've got some pretzels here if you want to take them."

We all turn and look at my mother, who has managed to sneak up on us like a ninja.

" 'S all right, Mrs. Hill," says Zoë. "Sally West lives right near the Kenmore Tavern, so we're going to stop in at Woolworths to pick up some soft drinks and bags of chips and stuff on our way."

"Okay. Well, I hope you all have a good time," says my mum.

*You and me both,* I think as I follow Zoë and Nick out the front door.

As soon as we get to the Kenmore Tavern Woolworths, we split up: Zoë to aisle 6 to get a few bags of corn chips, Nick to aisles 4 and 9 to get the dip and the latest edition of *Rugby League Week* and me to aisle 11 to get the soft drinks. We pool our money and arrange to regroup in no more than ten minutes outside Woolies.

Bottles in hand, I see Zoë at the express-lane register loaded up with far too much junk food. She turns her head and sees me staring and pokes her tongue out at me. I smile and hold up the bottles of soda. I look past her down the line of people and notice Nick isn't with her. I walk farther down past the magazine aisle and eventually spot him standing in the pasta aisle. With *Rugby League Week* jammed under his arm, he's busy reading one of the free Woolworths recipe cards. A card for béchamel sauce.

## THIRTY

Five minutes into the party and I'm really, seriously, not having a good time. I look around and count how many people are here. There's about fifteen—not including Zoë, Nick and myself. Not everyone has turned up. Louise, Natalie, Phil and Josh, who are all in Year 9 or 10, are sitting in front of the television watching reruns of *Magnum, P.I.* The Year 11s—Rowena, Clare, Angus, Charlie, Eva and the guy with dark hair who frequently whined about the lack of representation of "stage crews" in the yearbook—are outside laughing hysterically at some impersonation Angus is doing. Rowena, Charlie, Dark-Haired Weird Guy and Angus all have cigarettes in their hands, although Angus is the only one who appears to know what he's doing. The others look like they're faking it. The only other Year 12s here are Amanda

Towers, Leanne Suthers, Brad Fraser, Marty Davidson, Stacey McMaster and Kate Winter, who are all on the couches next to me, engaged in some kind of heated debate about the superiority of Prince over Michael Jackson. The phrase "rubber-hipped dance moves" is being bandied around a lot by Brad.

Nick McGowan is—as is his specialty—nowhere to be seen. This annoys me. I'm not sure why he even bothered to come.

I stick two stale Cheezels in my mouth. I'm not sure if it's a sad indictment of me or this party that I'd actually rather be at home memorizing Ophelia's "Hamlet's a nutter" speech. But then I've never been much of a party person. The last school party I went to was Louise Kaye's last October, out at Brookfield. Practically everyone in our grade went to that party. It was okay at first. The garage had been turned into a dance floor. There was a stack of food. The music was great. Christopher Jacks started doing some of his impersonations of the teachers at school and had everyone in fits of laughter. My mouth began to hurt from laughing so much. But a few hours later and the Kayes' bathroom smelled like vomit. And their backyard was full of spew, cigarette butts, discarded Passion Pop bottles and one or two couples having sex. Meanwhile, Louise was stressing out because someone had poured beer into her parents' pool. Naturally, everyone ignored her except some girl from choir. Christian East got into a fight with some girl from St. Margaret's who turned up uninvited. Natalie Swan was the worst, though. She vomited on herself and then, later, passed out on the dance floor with one of her boobs hanging out. What I remember about looking over at Natalie is that the song "Kick" by INXS was playing. It was like Alice stepped through the looking glass and into a Teen Binge Drinking commercial. Anyway, that's when I ended up sneaking to a phone and ringing Mum and Dad to come and pick me up early. Which is what I'd like to do right now. Not because this party is out of control—it's about as out of control as my nana. But because this party is boring, and I'd rather be at home memorizing Ophelia's babble or watching last week's taped episode of *21 Jump Street*. Or doing a dozen other things other than sitting here and eating stale Cheezels.

And then. And then Zoë, Sally and Amanda get their hands on some Bacardi rum and Cokes. I don't know where the alcohol came from. It could belong to Sally's parents, who are overseas, or to her brother, Tom, who's at a late uni lecture. Regardless, it's now being drunk by a group of high school kids. Zoë chugs hers through a straw and immediately goes out onto the deck (balancing the empty glass on her head) and offers to take her clothes off for five bucks. Accustomed to Zoë's frequent offers to strip, nobody pays any attention to her (except the Year 9s, who have started pooling their change). But Zoë is nothing if not persistent and won't be put off by the group's overall indifference to her offer of nudity. In her mind the issue is clearly fiscal, because she immediately drops her stripping fee to three dollars. Still no takers.

"How about a dollar?" she hollers while attempting to shimmy up against a rubber-tree plant.

Someone chucks a Cheezel at Zoë's head. Zoë, naturally, takes this as encouragement and in a bewildering move shoves the Cheezel down her pants, all the while singing her own slurred striptease music.

Just as I'm moving in to stop her from unbuttoning her shirt—or eating the Cheezel—she spots the Wests' fish tank and cries, "Fishies!" She dashes—all knees and elbows—to the lounge-room fish tank like a drunken gazelle. Then she collapses onto the beanbag and starts watching *Magnum, P.I.* reruns.

I'm less concerned about Zoë than I perhaps should be. But having seen my best friend display similar antics (sans Cheezel, plant and alcohol) at the Year 9 confirmation retreat three years ago, I'm not entirely convinced that Zoë is actually drunk. I think she just likes the *idea* of being drunk, and so long as there's no actual nudity and no vomit to clean up, I'm happy to go along with her faux-drunk routine. Still, it's probably time for me to get her some water.

Sally's house is pretty big, and it takes me a while to find the kitchen. It's one of those fancy kitchens with slate tiles and one of those big island counters in the middle of the floor and a fridge with double doors. I wonder what it must be like to come from a rich family, a family with an island in the kitchen. It takes me a while to find a glass (I find one with Muppet Babies on it!) and then to find my way back out to the group. As I round the corner of the lounge room, ready to give Zoë my "it's time to leave" speech, someone yells out, "There she is!" Another voice calls out, "Rachel!"

I turn, eyebrows raised. Everyone is sitting in a circle on the lounge-room floor. And there's a bottle in the middle of the circle.

Oh God. They're playing Spin the Bottle.

Leanne yells out, "C'mon!"

I reluctantly walk over to the group. That's when I notice Nick McGowan. He's back, sitting in the circle next to Kate Winter. Ready to play.

THIRTY-ONE

"We're not playing Spin the Bottle," Amanda says as she makes room for me to squash in between her and Angus. I am flooded with relief. "We're playing Truth or Dare." Her eyes light up in a way that doesn't exactly console me.

I hate Truth or Dare. But I take a seat beside Amanda because that's what's expected. My heartbeat begins to quicken.

There's a climate of anxiousness, almost fear, every time the bottle spins. Truth or Dare is a bit like watching *A Nightmare on Elm Street;* you really want to leave, but the excitement of staying keeps you pinned to your seat. As the bottle pinpoints victims, I watch as most people opt for truth since it is a well-known fact that dares could involve naked streaks. Clare is first. Brad asks for the truth about what exactly happened between her and Jacob Wellman at the Hoodoo Gurus concert at Expo 88 last year. (A: Kissing. With tongues. She let him put his hand up her shirt during the song "Like Wow— Wipeout.") Kate Winter's next. She's asked if she's still a virgin. (A: She pauses, says "Yeah" and then flashes a sly look to give the impression she's possibly lying . . . which means she probably is a virgin.) When it's Marty's turn, Clare asks him if he's gay. Marty laughs nervously but at the same time looks devastated. Then he says, "No. People always ask me that. I did have a girlfriend in Year 10, you know." I feel immediately sorry and embarrassed for him.

Marty takes his turn to spin, and I get a bad feeling in my stomach. It spins. And spins. And spins. And stops. At Nick McGowan.

Nick doesn't notice at first—he's talking to Kate Winter about something to do with the new Transvision Vamp album. But everyone else has noticed, and there is suddenly an atmosphere of expectation. It's a weird kind of atmosphere, as though everyone is holding their breath, waiting for what happens next. Because when it comes to truths, there are many unanswered questions and rumors hanging over Nick McGowan's head.

"McGowan, you're up," yells Angus across the circle.

Nick looks up, a little startled, as though he had momentarily forgotten where he was, only to realize he is sitting under a spotlight. He looks around the circle, the smile falling from his lips, and I watch his eyes move down to see that the bottle is indeed pointing at him. Nick's face goes pale.

"Truth or dare?" Angus's tone is laced with challenge.

All eyes volley back to Nick McGowan. Nick who isn't saying anything. And all I can think is, *I've got to do something. I've got to help him.*

"That bottle is totally borderline between Nick and Eva. Marty should spin it again."

Angus shoots me a withering look. "No way. Truth or dare, McGowan?" I watch Nick bite his lip and stare at the carpet.

"Fine," says Angus. "We'll go with truth. Is it true that over the Christmas holidays you—"

"Dare," says Nick.

Nick McGowan has chosen dare. You can almost see the disappointment, watch the crowd visually deflate. Shoulders relax. People lean back again, not forward. There will be no revelations tonight. Personally, I feel a combination of relief and disappointment. I want to know Nick's secrets. I'm just not sure I want everyone else to know at the same time.

"All right, I dare you to choose a girl from this circle to kiss for five minutes."

"Fine. But I'm not doing it in front of all of you. I'll kiss one of the girls for five minutes but in another room."

"He can do it in the study," says Sally excitedly,

pointing to a room off to the left while at the same time fiddling with her hair.

"It has to be on the mouth," says someone else. I'm not sure who. Possibly Marty.

Nick rolls his eyes at this and says, "Obviously."

"So who do you choose?" asks Angus.

The circle leans forward. I look over my shoulder at the TV and pretend to watch *Magnum, P.I.* even though the sound is down. My heart is in my throat.

"I choose Rachel."

THIRTY-TWO

Nick closes the study door behind him, shutting out the catcalls and cheering that accompanied our walk to this room.

"We've got five minutes."

I'm not sure if he's looking at me as he says this or not because I'm just leaning against the study wall, arms crossed and staring at the floor. My heart is beating so fast it feels like it's actually hitting my chest. Five minutes? Five minutes of what, exactly? I don't know if I'm excited or terrified at the thought of what lies ahead.

I never expected this. I so badly wanted him to choose me and so badly didn't want him to choose me, all at the same time.

And then it happened. "I choose Rachel." Not Zoë

or Amanda or Leanne or Kate Winter or any of the other girls. Nick had specifically requested me. And I have to admit that when he said my name, I got the same feeling in my stomach as when they announced me as a prefect late last year. Because he may be a pain and annoying and a million other things, but Nick Mc-Gowan is gorgeous, in a disheveled blond surfer kind of way.

Naturally, when he said my name, I played it cool and pretended to be disinterested. I rolled my eyes. I made a horrified face at the carpet. I definitely made sure I didn't look pleased. Or worse, enthusiastic. And then I looked at Zoë across the circle. Just from looking at her face, I'd know what she was thinking. Our eyes met. She nodded her approval.

So now I'm here with Nick. Alone. In a study at Sally West's house. With the door shut. And "Kokomo" by the Beach Boys is playing on the stereo outside.

"So . . ."

"So . . ."

"Thanks for going along with this." He smiles at me as though I'm here for a job interview. "And thanks for trying to help me out there."

"It's fine," I say, looking away and trying to keep the combined fear and excitement out of my voice. I wish I hadn't eaten quite so many Cheezels. Oh God. What if I taste like fake cheese stuff when he kisses me?

"What time is it now?"

I glance down at my watch. "Eight-forty-five." I try to say this in an alluring manner. Then I flick my hair a little bit and try to look seductive. But not slutty—I don't want him to think we're about to have five-minute sex. I look out the window and start singing along to "Kokomo" in a nonchalant, I'm-really-laid-back kind of way. I love this song.

"I hate this song," says Nick, with his back turned to me.

"Me too." I roll my eyes as if I'm completely over it while making a mental note to hide my "Kokomo" cassette when I get home.

I glance at Nick. He doesn't seem to be interested in me at all. He's too busy looking at the bookcase in Sally West's study. Pulling books out, reading the back-cover blurbs, putting them back.

"So how long do we have in here?" I say, trying to hurry him along. I know full well we've only got five minutes, but I want to get the ball rolling.

"Five minutes," he calls over his shoulder.

"So . . ." *Try to think of something to say. Say something. Say something.*

"So good idea suggesting that we come into this room."

He pushes a copy of *The Road Less Traveled* back into the bookcase. "Well, this way they won't know what we did."

What the hell does that mean? Suddenly I just want

to get this over and done with. "Well, I'm ready when-ever you are."

He turns around and looks at me with a puzzled expression.

*Oh shit.*

It's a horrible moment. One of those horrible moments when you immediately know that you've said the wrong thing. That you've just made a complete fool of yourself.

"We're not actually going to do anything, you know that, right? We're just going to tell them that we kissed, and they won't know the difference. You knew that, *right?*"

It takes a second for me to register the meaning of his words. *We can just tell them that we kissed. He has no intention of kissing me. Ohmygod, I'm such an idiot. I should have known. . . .*

"I knew you wouldn't be interested because of your boyfriend."

My brow furrows and then the penny drops. My boyfriend. I'd completely forgotten that in the library that day I'd told Nick McGowan I had a boyfriend.

"You *do* have a boyfriend, right?" Nick's face is mov-ing from puzzled to suspicious.

"Yes."

"That's what I thought."

Nick takes a seat in the swivel chair behind the desk. I slide down the wall and onto the carpet, rest my head on my knees and wait the next few minutes out. "Don't Worry, Be Happy" plays on the stereo outside.

"They've locked us in."

"What?"

Nick turns the doorknob but the door won't open. He pushes against it with his shoulder. Then he turns to me. "Those morons have pushed something heavy against the door." He shakes his head and rolls his eyes.

I hear them laughing outside.

I slide back down the wall onto the carpet. "Could this evening get any worse?"

Yes, apparently, because no sooner are those words out of my mouth than George Michael's "I Want Your Sex" comes booming through the stereo in Sally West's lounge.

*Ohmygod, I want to die.* I don't know where to look. My face heats up. So I stare down at the carpet.

Nick McGowan walks back across the room to sit on the big black leather swivel chair behind the mahogany desk.

"My God, you cross your arms a lot."

I look up.

"I've never met anyone who crosses their arms as much as you. It's really standoffish."

"Well, I'm stressed. I've got a lot on my mind."

"Like?"

"Like three assignments, and we've got a Biology

exam coming up, and tomorrow is my last chance to win the Party Hostess of the Year title at work. And I've got to win it."

"Do I even want to know what Party Hostess of the Year is?"

I make a sarcastic face at Nick. "It's a competition at the restaurant where I work. It's the award given to the person judged to give the best birthday parties."

"So, what, there's a prize? You could win money or something?"

"No, it's just, it's just a title. You don't get anything. Anyway, the point is that I've *got* to win it."

"Why?"

"Why what?"

"Why have you got to win it? Is that what you want to do? Do you want to work with little kids or something? Are you hoping that it will help you get a job?"

I snort. "No. I want to do Communications."

Nick McGowan looks surprised. "So-o-o what difference does it make if you win the award? What does it matter?"

"Well—"

"Hello, lovebirds."

We look up to see Kate Winter in the doorway. "They were sitting on opposite sides of the room," she yells out over her shoulder. "I knew he wouldn't kiss her."

She turns back and looks at us, a smug expression on

her face. I feel my cheeks go red. I feel embarrassed and humiliated, and for a second I feel like I might actually cry, until Nick McGowan gets up, taps Kate Winter on the shoulder and says, "Kate, you've got food in your teeth." Then he turns to me, offers me a hand up off the floor and says, "Let's go get something to eat."

THIRTY-THREE

We're standing in Sally West's kitchen, staring into her fridge.

"I don't think we should be going through their fridge. We should be in the pool with everyone else."

But Nick's not listening. He's too busy pushing past containers. "Yeah, but it's ninety degrees, I'm starving and we need something cold. Where's Benson when we need her?"

"Yuck. Who eats beets?" I pick up a can of beets that's sitting on a middle shelf. "They look the way they taste."

"Rachel, Rachel, Rachel—beets are the best part of any hamburger. In fact, I would go so far as to say that a hamburger is not truly a hamburger unless it has at least three"—he holds up three fingers to my face—"slices of beet on it."

I screw up my face and push his hand away. "Beets? You're joking, right?"

"No. I love the stuff. It's the sweetness of the beets combined with the salty flavor of the beef patty. Then there's the texture and the color. It's the whole aesthetic of it. Beets have a lot going for them."

"You're insane."

"One day, Rachel, if you're very, very lucky, I'll share with you my secret recipe for beet-and-hummus dip."

I pretend to gag and say, "I'd rather eat my own vomit" as he opens the freezer door and picks up a dark blue ice cream container.

"Aah, Double Chocolate Swirl ice cream. Now we're talkin'."

"I don't know about this."

"Stop panicking. Mr. and Mrs. West are overseas. They'll probably come back fat. We're doing them a favor." I follow him out the screen door to take a seat at the small cast-iron table and chairs on the patio.

I look down at the ice cream bucket. "But Sally and her brother are still here. This is probably theirs."

Through the screen I watch Stacey and Amanda walk into the kitchen and grab a box of chocolates out of the fridge. When they see Nick and me sitting out on the patio, they wave.

I wave back.

"See, they're doing it. They're raiding the fridge, too."

I turn back to Nick. "Stacey brought those choco-lates with her, fool."

He holds out a spoon and says, "Do you want some or not?"

I hear someone coughing and then wheezing inside.

"Hear that? That's smoker's cough. That'll be you someday, considering how much you smoke. You're such a—"

Suddenly there's a crash. Nick and I both turn our heads just in time to watch Amanda Towers collapse onto the slate tiles of the kitchen floor. And before I can even process what's happened, Nick has run inside.

Stacey has raced out of the room to fetch the phone, leaving Nick and me with Amanda, who is lying uncon-scious on the floor. Her face has suddenly become covered with a lumpy red rash, and her lips and tongue are swollen and blue, distorting her face.

"If Stacey's calling an ambulance, what are we sup-posed to do?" I turn and look at Nick McGowan, who is kneeling next to Amanda, talking out loud to himself.

"Dr. ABC, Dr. ABC. D is Danger. Is she in danger?" He looks around. "Okay, no." He adjusts Amanda's head so that she's lying completely flat on the kitchen floor. "R is . . . shit—what's R?"

He looks at me.

"I dunno. I dunno, Nick. You're the one who's done these courses. Maybe R is Recovery?"

"No. R is, R is, Response. R is Response. Amanda, can

you hear me?" I watch Nick McGowan shake Amanda gently by the shoulders. "Amanda? Okay, no response. No response." He runs his fingers through his hair and looks up at me. "I can't remember what to do. Six first-aid courses, and I can't remember anything."

"Yes you can."

He looks down at Amanda. "Okay, what does this look like? Lips and tongue swollen. Rash. This is like an allergic—" He spots a bracelet on her arm and bends closer to examine it. "This bracelet says she's allergic to peanuts. She must have accidentally eaten something with peanuts. Her throat is swelling up. She's gonna stop breathing soon. Dr. ABC, so *A* is Airways."

Stacey rushes back into the room. "An ambulance is coming. Five minutes."

"Did Amanda just eat something with peanuts?" I look at Stacey, unable to mask the panic in my voice.

"Well, we thought the chocolates we had were plain. But—"

Nick says, "Don't worry about that. Get her handbag. There'll be an EpiPen in her handbag. The bracelet indicates Amanda has medication with her all the time."

"Okay," I say.

"A *what* pen?" says Stacey.

But Nick's not listening to Stacey, he's talking to himself about Amanda's breath being very faint and something about a pistol grip. He tilts Amanda's head back, pinches her nose and says out loud, "Blow. Look. Listen. Feel. Okay. Okay. That's it. Let's go." I watch as

Nick McGowan starts to give Amanda Towers mouth-to-mouth.

"Handbag," says Nick between counts. "Get her handbag."

Stacey stands frozen, staring at Nick McGowan.

"Stacey, go and get her handbag. *Go!*"

Thirty seconds later Nick is instructing us to tip the contents of Amanda Tower's handbag onto the kitchen floor, telling us to look for something that looks like a cross between a mascara and a syringe.

I find the white-and-yellow EpiPen in a zipped compartment of her bag, and Nick wastes no time in ripping off the cap, pulling down Amanda's jeans and jabbing the needle into her thigh.

The doorbell goes.

Stacey says, "That'll be the ambulance." But Nick doesn't look up or even notice the others who have started to wander in from the pool. Instead, he just keeps a firm grip on Amanda's chin and keeps counting out the breaths.

THIRTY-FOUR

There's nothing quite like a guest going into anaphylactic shock to kill a party.

By ten-fifteen everyone's gone home. Not that they're too disappointed. They are, after all, armed with the news that "Nick McGowan gave Amanda Towers mouth-to-mouth and jammed a massive needle into her thigh."

When the two EMTs ran in, they took over from Nick, putting Amanda on a stretcher and asking Nick what he had done.

"You've done well, mate," said the younger one, whose name badge said JAY. "Good work."

But Nick just nodded. We followed them out and gave them Amanda's handbag and the phone number of her parents. And then fourteen cast and crew members from the 1988 production of *Lady Windermere's Fan* stood on the driveway and watched Amanda Towers be taken away in an ambulance. Someone said, "Good one, Dr. McGowan" and slapped Nick on the back. Someone else said, "Wait till she hears that Nick McGowan pulled down her jeans." Eventually they all filtered back inside. But Nick, Stacey, Zoë and I just sat there on the driveway, staring at the road.

On our way home through Kenmore, Nick walks a few meters ahead of Zoë and me, his body language making it clear he doesn't want to talk about the evening's event. Even though the EMTs assured him that Amanda would be fine and that she'd probably have an overnight at the Wesley or the Royal Brisbane Hospital just to be safe. She did, after all, have an enormous bruise on her head.

So at ten-thirty on Friday night the three of us meander down Bielby Road in silence. Well, except for Zoë, who every now and then whacks me in the ribs and whispers, "I can't believe you didn't kiss him."

THIRTY-FIVE

Fiona Curtis is doing Pass the Parcel.

I contemplate this latest information at nine on Saturday morning as I shove my shorts and T-shirt into one of the lockers and button up my brightly patterned clowny blouse in front of the crew-room mirror. Then I turn to Vivian Woo and ask her how she knows.

Vivian leans back into the doorway, ankles crossed, spins her work baseball cap on her finger (something I now consider to be her signature move) and says that Janine Howie told her. And that Janine was working front counter with Fiona yesterday and was standing right there when Fiona asked Simon if it was okay if she used her own Pass the Parcel during the parties. Apparently, she'd been in the storeroom and found two boxes of leftover Muppet Babies toys and games from last year's Muppet Babies meal-deal promotion. And she'd used these toys and wrapped up a parcel for her kids.

I must look shocked. Or pissed off. Or both, because Viv looks at me with sympathy and says, "I know. And it probably wasn't even her idea. It was probably Mrs. Westacott's." Then she says she has to go. She's on drive-thru and was due to clock on two minutes ago.

I stand there, alone, in the crew-room change room and think about what I've heard. It's ingenious, this idea. Kids *love* Pass the Parcel. And it shits all over my usual games of Tiggy and Red Rover. So now Fiona Curtis is letting the kids make their own sundaes *and* she's playing Pass the Parcel. And her aunt—who happens to be the big boss—is helping her. And what have I got? Nothing. I've got nothing. And for the first time I actually begin to think that Fiona Curtis is going to beat me. And not because she's better but because she's getting insider help.

I'm going to lose.

I can't lose.

I look at myself in the mirror.

"Pull yourself together," I say to my reflection. "Put last night out of your mind. Concentrate. You are the most popular clown in this restaurant. You are the person who gets requested for more parties than any other staff member. You are going to win this bloody competition."

And then I strap on my red nose and march out into the restaurant, ready to give the birthday party of my life.

• • •

I'm feeling supremely revved up and confident until I read my party profile sheet. I've got Brownies. Six eight-year-old Brownies. As I start setting up the party table at the back of the restaurant, I try and convince myself that this isn't a bad sign. Even though the last time I did a birthday party for Brownies it was like trying to entertain the Children of the Corn. They squealed. And bickered. And kicked. And the birthday girl, Brianna (an aggressive child who bore a startling resemblance to a bug), actually bit one of her guests during a game of Tiggy. But what I remember worst of all is that these Brownies refused to call me Rachel. Within the first few minutes they were insisting on giving me an Aboriginal name, like the ones they give their Brownie pack leaders. So for ninety minutes they got to call me Berri Berri or Burri Burri or something. And I got to call them stupid f*%#ing Brownies (if only in my mind) as I went hoarse asking them to "please stop drawing on the walls." And then to "please stop throwing pickles at each other." And finally to "please stop trying to start a campfire using the bark in the playground." When, for the twelfth time, Brianna asked me if I knew what my Aboriginal name meant, I guessed "clown with a mental illness."

But that was then and this is now. And there's a title at stake, goddammit.

*You can do this,* I think over and over while I wipe down the tables and blow up the balloons. *Do not be afraid of the Brownies. Do not be afraid of the Brownies.*

And then the Brownies arrive. And I am afraid of them. The birthday girl looks like she could take me. She's a little hefty for eight.

But today's Brownies are not the Brownies of last year. They are polite, non-fire-starting Brownies. The type of Brownies who laugh and giggle and Brownie-clap their way through the entire party. And as each minute ticks by, I realize that this is quite possibly the best party I have ever done. The kids are ecstatic. The parents are delighted. Nobody poos or goes into a peanut-induced coma. Everything runs like clockwork. Even Simon gives me two thumbs-up from the corner of the room, where he has been observing since the party began.

At the end of the party one of the mothers comes up and asks me if she can request me for her daughter's party next month. As I'm wiping some cake off the table, even Simon comes over, pats me on the back and says, "Good job."

But best of all, when I clock off, get changed and walk out of the restaurant, Nick McGowan is sitting on one of the tables outside, eating a burger.

# THIRTY-SIX

"Hey." I try to keep the happiness out of my voice. "I hope there were beets on that burger."

He shakes his head in mock disgust. "Only two slices—I think I'm gonna have to have a word with your manager."

"So how did it go?" He hops down off the table.

I shrug. "It was good, I think. It's hard to tell."

"But there was no poo at this one, right?"

"Right." We start to walk back home.

"Amanda's parents rang to thank us. And your parents are treating us to pizza tonight. And they're going to give us both money to go see a movie next week."

"I didn't do anything. It was all you, buddy."

He shrugs. "Well, you are second to none when it comes to emptying out a handbag in an emergency."

I smile.

"Anyway, Amanda's fine."

"God, wasn't it weird? It just all happened so quickly." I push the pedestrian-crossing button at the lights.

"Yeah."

"So how are you feeling about what happened?" I look to see the traffic slowing down.

"Don't say it."

"What?" I turn to look at Nick but he is staring at the traffic.

"You're wondering whether giving Amanda Towers mouth-to-mouth would make me want to study Medicine again, aren't you?" He looks at me.

I shrug.

"Well, it didn't. I mean, it was good to, you know, be able to do something. Help her. But . . ." He pauses. "The fact is it doesn't always go that way. Let's change the subject."

And so we do. We talk about all kinds of things on the walk home. All kinds of things not related to people having allergic reactions to chocolate-covered peanuts and having to be stabbed in the thigh with an EpiPen. We discuss why *Simon and Simon* is so much better than *Magnum, P.I.* The secret to a good béchamel sauce. Our thoughts on Biology. And as we walk, Nick laughs at my jokes and offers me sips of his Coke. And I'm thinking how great this is, how well Nick and I are getting along. Until he ruins it.

"You were actually prepared to kiss me, weren't you?"

"*What?*"

He turns to face me outside the post office on Marshall Lane. "In Sally's study last night. The more I think about it, the more I realize you were prepared to go along with it. At the beginning, when we first went in the study."

"No. I wasn't." I shake my head, walking away from him, as if this will make me sound and look more convincing.

"But you said, 'Ready when you are,'" Nick says, following me, nagging me the way Caitlin used to when she was little. "Why would you say that if you weren't thinking I was actually going to kiss you?"

"Yeah, well, 'Ready when you are' as in I was ready to start timing the five minutes. Whenever you were ready. To start timing," I say over my shoulder. "I didn't, don't, want to kiss you. I have a boyfriend. *Remember?*"

"That's right. The boyfriend I've never seen. So how is Snuffleupagus?"

"His name is Paul."

"How come Snuffy never calls the house? Rings you up? Are you, by any chance, the only one who can see him?"

"He does come to the house. He has called. He has."

"When? When has Snuffy called?"

"When you've been in the shower. Or outside smoking. And stop calling him Snuffy, for godsakes. His name is Paul. And we're going to see the Riptides tonight. Paul bought me the ticket. Because he's generous."

This is, of course, a lie. I'm going to the Riptides concert with Zoë.

"Really? So how long have you and 'Paul' "—he mimics quotation marks with his fingers—"been going out?"

"Three months." As I walk up the driveway, I start to fumble in my bag for the house keys.

"Where did you meet him?"

"Work," I shoot back. (What? *Ohmygod!*) "You know, I don't have to prove to you that I have a boyfriend. It's none of your business."

"Well, next time Snuffy rings, let me know. I'd like to say hello to him," he says as I open the front door. "Or maybe I'll just try and catch a glimpse of him tonight when he picks you up. Assuming he's not imaginary, of course."

"Fine. And for your information, he's visible now."

"Who? Who's visible?" I turn and look at Mum, who is walking out of the laundry folding some towels.

"No one. Nothing."

"Snuffleupagus," says Nick. "On *Sesame Street*."

"I thought Snuffleupagus was invisible?" asks Mum.

*What do either of you know about Snuffleupagus?* I want to scream. But I don't. Of course. Instead, I say,

"For godsakes, he wasn't invisible. He was real. But Big Bird was the only one who was ever around when he was there. So the others always thought that he was imaginary. But in 1985 everyone started seeing him. Okay?" I look at them both. "Can we drop this now, please?"

Mum pulls a face and goes back to folding the laundry. But as I walk off toward my bedroom, I hear Nick McGowan humming the *Sesame Street* theme song.

THIRTY-SEVEN

It's a relief to be going to the Riptides concert on Saturday night. Having spent the remainder of Saturday afternoon listening to Nick's Snuffy taunts, I just want to go out and get some fresh air, have some fun away from Nick. Nick who thinks I'm seeing the Riptides with Paul. I tell Nick that I am meeting Paul at the concert and instead arrange for Zoë to pick me up from outside my work restaurant when Nick is out with Dad renting a movie from Video Ezy. Zoë pulls into the restaurant car park driving her mother's orange Leyland P76, a car she likes to call the Steel Placenta. I'm not sure where Zoë got this name. Probably from her cousin Sharon, who's nineteen, very cool and drives a Commodore station wagon. But ever since Zoë got her license, she's started referring to the P76 as the Steel Placenta and making compilation tapes of her favorite driving music. Despite the fact the P76 doesn't have a tape deck. The most memorable was *Music from the Steel Placenta, Vol. 6*, which featured a lot of Indigo Girls and a disturbing dance version of Kenny Rogers's "The Gambler."

We pick up Katie Shew on our way and get to the university club a bit before eight p.m., even though the band isn't on until nine. We mill around and try to look like we belong in this crowd of mostly uni students. I am, of course, wearing completely the wrong thing: black stonewashed jeans and a Sydney Hard Rock Cafe T-shirt. And I have a scrunchie in my hair. It's just all so wrong. Zoë looks her usual casual cool—jeans, black T-shirt and a red bandanna in her hair. While Katie, as per usual, looks gorgeous. She's wearing a bubble skirt and a striped top with huge shoulder pads. She's well known for always wearing the trendiest clothes. And she looks way older than sixteen, which is why she has no trouble buying us all rum and Cokes. I take a sip and decide it's revolting, but I continue to sip it anyway, and only when Katie's back is turned do I tip my drink into a palm tree in the corner of the room.

It's nine-fifteen when the Riptides finally come on-stage, and as soon as they do, the whole vibe in the club changes. There's cheering and clapping and wolf whistling as the band members adjust their leads and microphones. Someone yells out, "Play 'Holiday Time'!" and someone else yells out something about the lineup at the bar being worse than the one at the New Zealand

Pavilion at Expo. The lead singer looks down at his guitar and seems to smile to himself and then turns his head and says something to the drummer. Then he turns back around and counts them in, and suddenly every inch of space in the club is filled with the opening chords of "Hearts and Flowers." (I recognize the song not because I'm a longtime Riptides fan like Zoë but because this particular tune was featured on *Music from the Steel Placenta, Vol. 2,* which Zoë made me listen to constantly last year.) As the Riptides play, it's like everyone in the room is suddenly in a good mood—intoxicated by the moment, beer in one hand and cigarette in the other, swaying and jostling and singing along. And I wonder if this, this music, this venue, this atmosphere that feels so foreign and intimidating to me now, will feel right to me next year when I'm a uni student. I hope so.

Katie leans into me and says something I can't quite hear.

"What?"

She pushes a strand of hair behind my right ear, leans a little closer and says, "I can smell marijuana!" I nod and say, "Me too," even though I'm not 100 percent sure what marijuana smells like. I feel something cold on my back and turn to see the back of a guy with spiky black hair wearing a Go-Betweens T-shirt stumbling his way through the crowd with two beers in his hands. Then I feel a tug on my hair and am confronted with Zoë's hand dangling my scrunchie in my face. She laughs. I try to snatch it back, but she slingshots it into the crowd and ruffles my messy permed hair with her hand. "Jesus," she yells, attempting to be heard above the music while dancing the twist at the same time. "It's as hot as a nun's nasty in here."

At the end of the first set Zoë wanders off in search of my scrunchie and Katie says she wants to have a D&M about Nick McGowan. I must look confused because she says, "You know, a *Deep and Meaningful*?"

"Oh, right."

She leads us to a quiet area near the girls' toilets.

"So what's it like having him live at your house?"

"Well, it's been sort of weird, I guess, but . . ."

"I mean, God, he's gorgeous. Jillian Powter and I were saying just yesterday that he seriously has the best body out of every guy in our year. I can't believe he's from Mount Isa, because——"

"Middlemount. He's from Middlemount."

But Katie isn't listening. "Because he totally looks like a surfer. Don't ya reckon? God, I had the biggest crush on him last year when he joined my Legal Studies class. He always used to sit by the back window, so I started sitting there. I mean, it was totally obvious I liked him 'cause I was always asking him questions and stuff, and——" She suddenly grabs my elbow. "You're not going to tell him any of this, are you? Promise me you won't tell him. . . ."

"No, I won't. I prom——"

"So has anything happened?" She leans in closer. "Have you kissed him?"

I decide not to tell Katie about the awkward events of last night's Truth or Dare game and instead keep my answers brief, just saying that Nick and I tend to keep out of each other's way, which isn't a total lie. But Katie is visibly disappointed.

"So nothing's happened?"

I shake my head and look over toward the stage. "Nope."

"So what do you reckon about the rumors that are going around about what he did to himself over the summer holidays, because—"

That's when I get hit in the face with my pink-and-purple scrunchie. Katie bends down to pick it up off the floor, and I scan the crowd, grateful to spot a grinning Zoë walking toward us just as the Riptides are stepping back out onstage.

It's eleven-thirty p.m. when Zoë drops me home.

I walk up the driveway, thankful that Mum has left a few lights on for me so that I can navigate my way through the dark to my bedroom. I turn the lock and then wave to Zoë—we have a rule that you don't drive away until the other person has safely opened their front door. She waves back and I watch as she drives the Steel Placenta off into the night, winding its way through the streets of downtown Kenmore. I turn back to the door and gently push it open, stepping softly into the house so as not to wake anyone up. I wonder what will happen between Nick and me tomorrow.

"So did you have a good time?"

I gasp in fright, turn and, squinting, see Nick McGowan sitting on the lounge.

I walk toward his silhouette. "What are you doing?" I say this in the sternest whisper I can muster.

He whispers back, "We need to talk."

THIRTY-EIGHT

My mind is reeling as I follow Nick down to his room. He wants to talk in there, he says, because it's private. No one else can hear. We can talk more freely.

"Okay," I say. So many things are going through my head. He's going to confess that he has a crush on me. I let myself think how great that would be. I bet that's not it. Or. Or he knows that Paul is made-up. Or. Or he's done something. Snooped through my room. Found my diary and photocopied it for the boys at school. And he wants to confess. Or he's moving to another family's house. He's miserable here. Has been complaining about it to Mrs. Ramsay and she's finally sick of his moaning and is sending him to live with another family. A family who don't watch *It's a Knockout*.

"Rachel?"

I look up.

"You can take a seat, you know. And don't look so scared. It's all okay."

I perch myself on the edge of his bed. Nick sits next to me.

My mouth has gone dry. I really need a glass of water.

"So what do you want to talk about?" (I'll just say that the Paul/Snuffy thing got out of hand and that it was a joke from the start. Zoë and I just never expected him to be so gullible and fall for it.)

He takes my hand in his.

*Oh God.*

"I just want you to know that I know. And it's totally fine by me."

"Know what?" (That I like him? That Paul is fake? That I snooped in his room and found those brochures?)

"I can't imagine how hard this has been—still is—for you. And I'd like to think that we're friends. I want you to know that I am *totally* cool with it. Really. So you and Zoë should feel comfortable around me."

"*What?* Nick, what are you talking about?"

"It's okay. Rachel, it's me, Nick. You don't have to lie about it any longer."

"Lie about what?"

"About you and Zoë being gay. Being, you know, together. I'm totally cool with it."

He thinks I'm a lesbian.

"You think I'm a lesbian? You think I'm a *lesbian*? *I am not a lesbian, Nick!*"

But Nick isn't listening. To him I'm just some hysterical homosexual sitting on the edge of his bed.

"I saw Zoë drop you off tonight. That's when I knew. You weren't out with Paul because there is no Paul. 'Paul' is actually Zoë. And, I mean, it's totally understandable, because you're worried about breaking the news to your parents."

"Nick. Nick." I start to shake his shoulders. "I am not gay. I am not gay. I'm not. Paul is made-up, that's true. There is no Paul. But Zoë and I are just—we're friends. I've known her since I was five years old. She's like a sister to me. I love her but I don't, you know, *lurve* her."

"I was worried you were going to do this."

"What?" My voice is now going into that dangerously hysterical zone.

"Deny it."

I stand up. *"I am not gay!"*

"So what you're saying is you're not gay? You and Zoë aren't a secret couple?"

"No. No, we are not."

"And Paul is . . ."

"Made-up. I wanted you to think that I had a boyfriend. But I'm straight. Really."

And that's when Nick says, "I thought so. I just wanted to hear you admit that Paul was fake."

With that he gets up from the bed, winks at me and says, "See you in the morning."

And I wander out of his room dazed, fighting the urge to throw up.

THIRTY-NINE

I successfully avoid seeing Nick McGowan for most of Sunday by staying in my room. I'm too humiliated to face him. So I stay upstairs and start work on my French assignment, wondering what the fallout is going to be from last night's revelation. Is he going to spread it around school that I had an imaginary boyfriend? I try not to think about it. That's probably what he'll do. He'll tell everyone that I made up a boyfriend to look cool.

I ring Zoë to tell her about last night's startling events—the trap that Nick planted by telling me he thought she and I were gay lovers. Zoë takes the news surprisingly well and doesn't seem the least bit fazed by Nick questioning her sexual orientation. Instead, her initial response is to say, "As if I'd date you! Give me some credit. For starters, you have crap taste in music, and then—"

"Forget the gay thing. It was a trick," I say, cutting her off. "A trick. To get me to tell him that Snuffy was made up. And now it really does look like I like him."

"Who's Snuffy?"

"Paul."

"When did you change your boyfriend's name to Snuffy? I mean, Rach, as if anyone is going to believe that you've been dating a guy called Snuffy."

"Zoë, focus! The point is that now Nick McGowan probably thinks I like him."

"But you do like him."

"But I don't *like him* like him."

She says, "Oh please" and then hangs up.

Half an hour later Mum knocks on my door. She's decided to make spaghetti Bolognese for dinner. "We're all eating too much takeaway," she says. "No more Kentucky Fried." After much pleading she allows me to eat mine in my room (since I tell her I'm doing an assignment). But she draws the line at letting me get out of doing the washing-up.

"You've got Nick to help you. It won't take you long."

Apparently, washing-up has become one of my new jobs. I roll my eyes and trudge downstairs, not caring that I'm wearing track pants and an old Sportsgirl T-shirt.

At the sink neither Nick nor I speak. I'm too embarrassed to even look at him since he now knows my love life is nothing more than imaginary. The silence between us starts to get uncomfortable as he puts the plug in and turns the taps on.

"I think we should play that game."

I feel him look at me. I say nothing.

"What was it called? Best Ever Feelings or something?"

I still don't respond.

"No, it was Best Free Feelings. Okay, a best free feeling." He pauses for a moment. "Okay, how about the feeling when you're driving down a rough dirt road and then you move onto smooth pavement. Rough to smooth, that's a great feeling. So what do I get now? Five points or something?"

He looks at me. I keep my head down.

"Come on, Rachel. Don't make me call your dad." He nudges me in the ribs. "If you play this game, I promise to do the washing-up by myself for the rest of the week."

I look at him, eyebrows raised.

"Really."

"Fine, but for starters you don't get points. There are no points in this game. You're just supposed to keep taking turns until someone gets stuck or gives up."

"Fine. Bring it on, Hostess Girl."

I look out the window and think for a minute. "Okay. The feeling you get when your name is called out and you've won an award you weren't expecting."

Now it's Nick's turn to raise his eyebrows at me.

"What?" I ask him.

"Is that *all* you think about? Winning stuff? Getting high grades? Beating everyone else? You're, like, obsessed with it."

"I am not."

"Whatever you reckon." He hands me a clean plate to dry.

"Fine." I give Nick my best sarcastic smile, take the plate and, while I'm drying it, say, "The best free feeling is when the person you hate more than anyone else in the world—who is arrogant and thinks that everyone is in love with him—is doing the washing-up and you get to tell him that he missed a bit."

I hand the plate back.

I watch Nick turn the plate over. "Where? It's perfectly clean."

"Let me see." I take the plate back from him, then I grab the spoon that's still sitting in the leftover spaghetti sauce and I pour a spoonful of sauce down the plate. "There," I say, pointing to the dribble of meat sauce.

Nick's mouth drops open. Then his eyes narrow.

Uh-oh.

Suddenly my hand is being shoved into the bowl of cold meat sauce. "Or that great feeling of putting your hand into a tub of cold Bolognese sauce. That's a special feeling," says Nick.

I yelp, trying to pull my hand out, but Nick forces it down, so that I'm now wrist-deep in Bolognese. I feel bits of mince and tomato squelching between my fingers.

"Having fun, you two?"

We both turn and see my father, looking somewhat bemused, in the kitchen.

Nick bites his lip. I attempt to remove my hand from the bowl but Nick is still holding it down. So I stand on his foot.

"Sorry." He releases his grip. I remove my hand.

I whisper through the side of my mouth, "The feeling of joy you get watching your worst enemy get caught by an adult."

Dad just looks at us, shakes his head and says, "Thank God you two didn't make dinner." He lingers in the kitchen, making him and Mum a cup of tea, forcing Nick and me to continue the washing-up in a more traditional, civilized fashion. But when Dad's back is turned, I flick some suds at Nick.

He laughs and knocks into me with his shoulder. I roll my eyes, try not to smile and start to dry the next plate.

Just after eleven p.m. our phone starts ringing. I hear the shuffle of my father's slippers and the murmur of voices in the kitchen. I lie there with my eyes closed, thinking that it's probably Caitlin. She never works out the time difference between France and Australia. She has a habit of ringing at all times of the day or night.

I tell myself to go back to sleep. Until I hear Nick McGowan's voice.

I stand at the top of the stairs, bleary-eyed. "Who's on the phone?"

"Go back to bed," says Mum.

I take a few steps down the stairs and see Nick McGowan sitting on the lounge-room floor, his back to me as he leans up against the couch, talking to someone on the phone.

I turn back to Mum. "Who's he talking to? Has something happened?"

I watch Mum shoot a glance at my dad, who says, "Everything is fine, Rachel. Go back to bed. It's just someone for Nick."

"Who?"

They walk toward me like two people paid to do crowd control.

"His friend Sam." They keep walking toward me, moving me backward. Back to bed.

"Why are they ringing now? What's happened?"

"It's fine, Rachel. We'll talk about it in the morning. Go back to bed."

I scratch my nose. "My hand smells like Bolognese," I say to no one in particular.

"Off you go, Rachel."

I turn to leave and head back up the stairs. As I pass Dad's study, I see the cordless phone sitting on his desk. I can solve this mystery once and for all.

I hold my breath as I put the receiver to my ear.

"It's all right, mate. You know you can ring me whenever you want."

Nick's voice has taken on a soothing tone—it takes me by surprise.

But it's what I hear next that makes my jaw drop. The sound of a little girl's voice whispering back, "Nick, when are you coming home?"

# FORTY

"Do you have a daughter?"

Nick's eyes spring open. "Holy shit! Rachel! What are you doing?"

"I want to know if you have a daughter?"

"At one o'clock in the morning? Jesus, how long have you been standing next to my bed?"

"Oh, get over it. I just got here. Is Sam your daughter? Yes or no?"

Nick sits up and mumbles something about the fact that he has a German excursion tomorrow and that at this rate he's going to sleep through his alarm.

"Well?"

"Sam's eight years old. I would've had to have fathered her when I was ten."

*"Yes or no?"*

"Jesus! No. *Obviously.* Do you think, maybe, we could talk about this in daylight hours?"

"She didn't sound eight, she sounded five."

"Well, she's eight. Eight going on forty-two." He rubs his eyes. Then he looks up at me. "What do you mean 'didn't sound eight'? Were you eavesdropping on our phone call? God, it's like you think you're from the CIA or something."

"I just want to know who she is. I want to know why there's so much mystery around who she is."

"What mystery? There's no mystery."

"Well then, why don't you ever say *who* she is? Hey?" I start to pace around his room. "If there's no mystery, why do you keep it such a secret? And why is some lit-tle kid ringing you all the time—including now, in the middle of the night?"

"It's not a secret, Rachel, you've just never asked me. If you wanted to know who Sam was this whole time, I would have told you. What is it with people? Nobody wants to ask anything direct. They just prefer to make up stupid rumors and spread them behind your back."

"Well, I'm asking. Who is Sam?"

He lets out a heavy sigh and says, "Sam is my best friend's little sister."

FORTY-ONE

And that's when Nick McGowan tells me what happened over the summer.

"Two weeks before the end of school last year, during our exam period . . ." He stops, then sighs and looks out the window. "Two weeks before the end of school last year, during our exam period, my best mate, Jason, decided to drive into Emerald in his dad's new Holden truck. It's about a two-hour drive from Middlemount and . . . aah . . ." He gives a half laugh and rubs his eyes. "I don't know why I'm even telling you that because it's irrelevant. Anyway, on the drive home—and the road is fairly straight and flat for most of the journey, right?" He glances at me then. I nod, trying to keep up with what he's saying. "So he's driving home from Emerald, and there's apparently just one car on the other side of the road traveling in the other direction. It's being driven by some old guy. Anyway, what happens is this old guy has a heart attack behind the wheel. He has a heart attack just when Jason's car is approaching in the opposite direction. So this old bloke's car swerves and crosses the double line—"

My stomach drops.

Nick looks at me, runs his fingers through his hair and then returns his gaze to the darkness beyond the window. "And the old bloke's car collides with Jason's truck." He nods. "They were both killed instantly."

*"Ohmygod."*

"Yeah." He turns to look at me for a moment. "So my best friend gets killed in a car accident, and Mike the police officer gets called, and the on-call doctor gets called, but nobody calls me. I'm his best friend. His *best* friend. I have known Jason Wilks since I was two years old. And you know why nobody rang me that day—or the day after, or the day after that—and told me that my best friend had died? Because my dad told them not to because I was in the middle of exam week in Brisbane."

Nick looks down at the floor and shakes his head. I'm at a loss for words. "That's what Dad told Mr. Wilks. He actually told them not to tell me because I was in the middle of exams and I needed to do well to get into Medicine. So the morning that my best friend's coffin was being lowered into the ground, I was sitting in a room in D-Block answering essay questions about *The Great Gatsby*. Sitting in an exam and later wondering whether I'd have the boarders' sandwiches for lunch or go and get a meat pie from the cafeteria."

Nick's eyes have become glassy pools of water, and I watch as he tips his head back and looks at the ceiling—but the tears run down his cheeks regardless.

"And I know why Dad did it, you know, I get that. I get that, but he should have told me. *He should have told me.*" He glances down at me and I nod, pushing tears from my eyes.

"See? Do you understand now what I've been trying to say to you? Life can just be ripped from you. And you know why Jason had gone to Emerald that afternoon? To get me a birthday present. That's why he was in the car. *I am the reason* Jason was in the car. And, see, I've thought about it, and I can't think of another time when he's done that before, driven into Emerald on a weekday after school."

I lean toward him, try to take his hand. "Yeah, but, Nick, you can't—"

He shakes his hand out of my grip. "You don't get it. You don't understand. When I came to Brisbane last year, I promised him I would keep in touch," he says, staring at the wall in front of him. "And I didn't. I didn't keep in touch. And I'd promised him that I'd go home for the weekend of the Rugby League Grand Final and I didn't go. I backed out on him at the last minute because Mr. Tallon wanted me to attend some pointless leaders breakfast.

"At Parliament House." I remember that breakfast. I was pissed off because I didn't get chosen to go.

He looks at me and shakes his head.

"I was just so caught up in all that school stuff—the awards and the grades. And he was my best friend. And this is the thing, Rachel. Life can just be taken away like that." He snaps his fingers. "He was my *best friend*. So all this shit about planning our futures is pointless. Jason was planning *his* future. He wanted to be a mechanic, own his own garage. He'd already set up an apprenticeship with a guy in Rocky. Fat lot of good that did him. He didn't get up that morning thinking, *I wonder if I'm going to be killed in a freak road accident today.* And I was already losing interest in becoming a doctor—I just didn't have the heart to tell my dad. But this settled it. It made me realize that there's no point in doing Medicine if doctors can't even save people when they really need it. There's no point."

I don't know what to say, don't know how to respond to any of this.

"And now everyone's concerned about me. Dad, Mrs. Ramsay, Mr. Tallon, Mr. and Mrs. Wilks. Dad thinks everything will be solved if I just go on Prozac. They want to medicate me up to the eyeballs. And they're all scared, you know, that I'm going to do something to myself." He turns and looks at me directly. "I'm not going to do anything to myself. I know what they're saying about me at school, but I've never even considered it, Rachel. Not for a second."

This time he lets me take his hand and I nod.

But then he's up, pacing the room, rambling about life being too short, how nothing matters and what a shit friend he's been.

I try to tell him that's not true.

"No, nope, I've just got to face the truth, and the truth is I failed my best friend when he needed me most. And that's just something I'll have to live with."

He wipes his eyes and sits back down. "Jase'd be calling me the biggest girl and giving me so much shit if he saw me now." He gives a half laugh.

"So tell me about Sam," I say. "How does she fit into all of this?"

"Right, right," he says, nodding and looking at the floor. "Sam is Jason's little sister. That first time she called was a bit of a shock because I've barely spoken to her since the accident. But now I tell her to ring whenever she wants. Your parents said it was okay, and most of the time she just wants to talk about Jase. What he'd be doing today. Like watching M*A*S*H. Or hogging the Atari. Or building those stupid model planes that he was so obsessed with. Tonight she dreamed she saw Jason sitting at her desk. Apparently, Jase reminded her to keep training Tads, their border collie, to shake hands, because pretty soon he'd do it. And he told her that he was sorry for leaving her. And that it was nobody's fault. And that he was with her, watching over her, watching over all of us, all the time. That's why Sam called at eleven p.m. She'd wanted to tell me about the dream."

"Wow."

For a moment we sit in silence. Eventually, I turn to him and say, "Do you believe in God?"

His eyes narrow for a moment and he stares at me for a while. Stares in a rather intense way, like a doctor looking at a troubling X-ray. Then he looks out the window and says in a voice like shattered glass, "Only in storms."

We stay up till three a.m. talking about Jason and Sam and school and parents. Talking about expectations and careers and Party Hostess titles and life after school and life after death. We talk about how someone ends up with Dog as a nickname. How Nick's father broke the news to him about Jason on the drive home from the Emerald Airport at Christmas. How Mr. McGowan just wants Nick to "reach his potential."

We don't come to any real conclusions. We don't have any epiphanies about the meaning of life or why we're all here. We just agree that life is random and hard. And sometimes it can feel like you're barely treading water.

## FORTY-TWO

Monday doesn't go the way I expect. When I get up, I look for Nick. I feel closer to him now, and I want to see him and acknowledge what happened last night. But Nick has gone. Already left for school.

"He got the early bus," says Mum, folding some laundry. "The German excursion bus was leaving at seven a.m. Now whose black sock is this?"

I walk through the gates at eight-thirty a.m.—just in time to see a certain Zoë Budd saunter through the front gates wearing dark sunglasses, loudly cursing the sun's excruciating glare. During English she complains— loudly—about having a headache. During Modern History she shushes people and asks Mrs. Finemore if she could keep her voice down. Mrs. Finemore responds by telling Zoë that she will not keep her voice down and that she will confiscate her sunglasses if she does not take them off immediately.

Zoë—allegedly—has a hangover from the party on Friday night. A delayed hangover that has taken three days to kick in. A hangover on time-lapse.

During morning tea, sitting out on the grass, I tell Zoë that she is being ridiculous. She cannot possibly have a hangover on a Monday from a party on Friday night. But it's hard to tell if she's listening because she's lying down, with her head in my lap and an eye pillow on her eyes. As soon as I start talking, her left hand signals me to stop. So I sit there, leaning against the wall of the Science Block, thinking about Nick and last night's revelation.

By eleven-thirty a.m. the school is buzzing with news that Zoë Budd has a three-day-old hangover and that Sally West had a party on Friday night that got kind of out of hand.

By one p.m. people are asking me if it's true that I "got with" Nick McGowan in Sally West's study.

By two p.m. the word is out that Nick McGowan saved somebody's life.

FORTY-THREE

Nick's at the front door, searching his backpack, when I walk up the driveway.

"Hey. Can't find my keys."

I hold up mine. "Anyway, looks like Mum and Dad are both home." I nod toward the garage. "You should've just knocked. Which bus did you get? I didn't see you on the bus."

"None. Di Randall's mother dropped me here. They live on Chapel Hill Road."

"How was the excursion? Where'd you go?" I turn the key in the lock and push open the front door.

Mum and Dad are standing in the kitchen. Waiting for us. And there's a plate of chocolate chip cookies staring at me from the counter.

"We know what you've done," says my dad. "Do you want to start explaining?"

"Not really," I say in a jokey tone, but neither of my parents smiles.

"Clearly, there has been some sort of cover-up going on."

I look at Nick. He looks at me. Suddenly he starts talking.

"Mr. and Mrs. Hill, Rachel had nothing to do with it. It was my fault. I just, uh, I don't want to do Medicine anymore, and so I decided that the only way to get through to him—you know, my dad—was to drop down to Math in Society. There was a consent form. So I forged your signatures. And Rachel, I swear, knew nothing about it."

My mum looks confused and says, "I'm lost."

Dad says, "What has this got to do with the huge scratch we found today on your mother's car?"

And then I look at Nick and say, "We're dead."

Dad goes on and on about how disappointed he is in both of us, how Nick's father and the school will have to be informed.

Nick's on the phone for the rest of the night. To his dad. Then to Mrs. Ramsay. Then to his dad again. I barely get to see him to ask him why he took all the blame for the forged form and to thank him. Instead, Mum and Dad pile me up with chores, and Nick stays in his room, on the phone.

As I clean out Gipper's cage, I silently ask God to not let him leave—that if he lets Nick stay, I'll promise to start listening in Chapel every morning. And that I'll do the 40 Hour Famine every year for the rest of my life. But it's hard to tell if God's even listening. Or cares. I begin to wonder if I'd have more success consulting Zoë's Psychic Lettuce. I do the washing-up alone, wondering if Nick is downstairs packing.

**FORTY-FOUR**

"Can you zip me up?"

I look up. Fiona Curtis is looking over her shoulder at me while at the same time struggling with the back zipper of her rainbow-striped polyester clown top. "These tops are just so ugly. We look like human beach balls."

I smile weakly and zip her up.

"Thanks," she says, strapping on her red nose. "Are you okay? You seem kind of distracted."

"I'm just . . ."

"Worried about how we're going to manage twenty eight-year-old kids? Me too. But with two of us in charge, I figure we'll be all right. I'll just go and get the place mats. Your wig's crooked, by the way."

I watch her go—the human exclamation mark. I can't believe I've been rostered on to do a party with my nemesis. And they haven't even told us who won the Party Hostess title—although Vivian Woo reckons we're finding out on Thursday. I stand and look at myself in the mirror. Fiona Curtis is right. My wig is crooked. But I don't care. I don't want to be here today, right now, doing this stupid party with these stupid kids. I want to be with Nick.

I rip open a packet of short red birthday candles and start to jam them, one by one, into the multi-colored ice cream cake that Fiona has brought out from the freezer. I haven't seen Nick since last night. He didn't get the bus with me this morning. And today he hasn't been in class. Zoë reckons that at midday, when she walked past Mrs. Ramsay's office window, she saw Nick inside with some old, fat bloke who might have been his dad. And I just want to know what's going on, what everyone is saying— whether they're going to expel him or suspend him. Or just move him to another family where the father's signature is a little harder to forge on forms and where the daughter isn't a willing accomplice.

And that's when it occurs to me that the truth is I've gotten pretty used to having Nick McGowan around.

I put the cake back in the freezer. Fiona walks back into the room with a big grin on her big clowny face and says, "They're here. We're on."

The party is a shock to me. Not because it's mayhem, as you'd expect with twenty eight-year-old kids all high on Coke and ice cream cake. It's a shock because of how smoothly it runs. And as hard as it is for me to admit, it's all thanks to Fiona. As I hand out the burgers and fries and fetch the drinks, Fiona has the kids wrapped around her little finger. She tells them jokes and makes them laugh and remembers all their names. Just when the kids are getting bored with Simon Says, she whips out a tape deck, puts on some Ratcat and plays a dancing game called Bob and Freeze. The kids love it. I love it. Fiona Curtis is like some kind of freak Mary Poppins clone dressed in a clown outfit.

When the kids are busy eating their burgers, I turn to her and say, "I thought I was good, but you're incredible. These kids just love you. How do you do it?"

Fiona laughs and shrugs and says, "Dunno. I want to do Primary-School Teaching next year. I always just loved being with kids."

That's when I find myself saying, "You deserve to win the Party Hostess title. I really hope you win it."

Fiona Curtis smiles at me. "Thanks."

Some freckly kid asks for another lemonade.

"I'll fetch it," I say to Fiona. "You stay here and entertain them."

I move to leave and then stop and turn around to face Fiona.

"Is it true that you're related to Mrs. Westacott? That she's your aunt?"

Fiona looks suitably horrified. "What? No, she was our neighbor at Brookfield, but that was years ago. Now we live in Moggill."

"Right," I say, and go and fetch more drinks.

## FORTY-FIVE

Fiona is hugging all the kids goodbye when I'm wiping down the tables. And that's when I look up and see Nick McGowan sitting on the restaurant fence outside, watching me through the window.

I walk outside.

"You never told me you were a twin," he says, glancing over at Fiona. "It's so cute how you two dress the same."

I roll my eyes and pretend to laugh and say, "Yeah, very funny. Actually, FYI, that's Fiona Curtis."

"Really?" He takes another studied look at Fiona, who is still hugging kids goodbye. "So did you whip her ass? Is the Party Clown crown yours?"

I shrug. "Dunno. Probably not. I don't really care

anymore. She's actually very good—better than me. Imagine that."

He laughs. "Imagine that." And that's when Nick McGowan jumps down from the fence and stands in front of me.

"I didn't see you at school today." I give Nick a playful punch in the arm.

"Yeah, well, that's sorta why I'm here. There's trouble in Denmark."

I feel sick.

"What? What do you mean?"

"Dad's here." He glances over at a Yellow Cab waiting in the car park. "He got the first plane down here this morning, and now he's taking me back home. The school has been really good. They were prepared to let me stay, but Dad and Mrs. Ramsay think it would be better if I went back with him. To sort some stuff out. Do a bit of counseling. You know."

I nod and look down at the ground, not wanting Nick McGowan to see the tears filling my eyes.

"The good news is that I think my dad finally gets that I don't want to do Medicine."

I nod and mumble, "That's good."

"Yeah. Yeah, it is, but I, uh, told Dad that I couldn't go without saying goodbye to you."

I laugh and sniff and wipe the teardrops from my face. "For what it's worth, I'm really glad you came to live with us."

And then Nick McGowan shoves a badly wrapped

present in my hands and kisses my cheek and whispers, "I really wish I'd kissed you at that party."

And the next thing I know, he's walking away, toward the cab. Nick McGowan turns back around and says, "Best free feeling in the world: changing schools one week before the compulsory five-kilometer cross-country!"

He laughs and waves, and I watch as he gets into the waiting cab.

With the taxi out of sight, I open the card first. It's a picture of a freaky circus clown. Inside, Nick's written, "You in twenty years? Rachel, you're the beets on my hamburger. Nick."

I rip open my present and find two bright pink washing-up gloves. And Nick's recipe for beet-and-hummus dip.

I laugh out loud.

"Who was that? He was totally hot." I turn and see Vivian Woo emptying the restaurant bin. "And why'd he give you washing-up gloves?"

I look at the gloves, smile to myself and say, "It's a private joke between Nick and me. You wouldn't understand."

EPILOGUE

Rumors started going around again about Nick McGowan pretty much as soon as he left our school that March. Rumors that my parents had found drugs in his room. Rumors that Nick and I had been caught having sex by the pool. Rumors that he was on suicide watch in a funny farm in Rockhampton.

The truth is that Nick left Brisbane that day and started the following week as a weekly boarder at St. Brendan's in Yeppoon. Close enough so that he could go home to Middlemount on weekends, far enough away that he didn't have to sit through Sam's daily ballet concerts in her backyard.

He never did change his mind about not wanting to be a doctor. Nick McGowan decided he wanted to be a chef instead and maybe open his own restaurant one day.

A restaurant that specializes in lasagna and never puts less than three slices of beet on a hamburger. So these days, while I'm still battling first-year uni nerves and trying to navigate my way around campus, Nick's training as an apprentice chef for a guy called Mario in a little Italian café on Merthyr Road in New Farm. Which is all well and good, but just yesterday I met him at Dooleys Hotel and had to take the pool cue out of his hand, reminding him that he'd promised to make me dinner. After he bought me a beer. We still debate the role of beets on a hamburger.

Nick McGowan came to stay with my family for only a few weeks in 1989, but it was enough time for me to realize that sometimes change is a good thing. That when you're looking for the truth, it's always better to go to the source. That life isn't always better with a Party Hostess crown on your head.

And that the best free feeling in the world is when you find a new friend who you know you'll have with you for the rest of your life.

ACKNOWLEDGMENTS

Thanks to my family and friends in Australia, who supported me (and kept feeding me chocolate) while I wrote this novel. Couldn't have done it without you.

Three cheers for my UQP family: Greg Bain, Taressa Brennan, Simone Bird, Leonie Tyle and—most of all—the fabulous (and patient) Madonna Duffy. Eternal gratitude to my editor Rachel Scully, who shone the torch when I was stumbling around in the dark. A round of applause also must go to my American team, including David Forrer (for introducing me to gawker.com and for being part of the world's best business lunch at Thalia in NYC), my wonderful agent Catherine Drayton, who believed in this story from the first moment I told her about it, and my fabulous editor Erin Clarke, for taking a chance on yet another Aussie. Erin,

I'll "shout" you a beer next time I'm in the Big Apple. Thanks also to Jack for giving this story the thumbs-up.

And finally, thanks to Brad—for the consistently fabulous sang choy bow, for telling me how to beat his serve on the tennis court after that fourth ace and for always telling me how much he believes in me and my writing.

This book is unofficially dedicated to the staff and students of Middlemount Community School, who welcomed me with open arms in the summer of 2004.

AUTHOR BIO

Rebecca Sparrow spent most of 1980 running around her family's backyard wearing a bathing suit and her mother's high heels, armed with a Super Soaker. In her yearlong reign of terror, she arrested her dog, Mac, 329 times. Rebecca graduated to selling touch lamps and working as a nanny, a travel writer, a television publicist, a marketing executive, a magazine editor and a secret shopper (once). She currently writes for the Australian newspaper the *Courier-Mail* and is an ambassador of War Child Australia, an international organization dedicated to providing immediate, effective and sustainable aid to children affected by war. Her first novel, *The Girl Most Likely,* is in development as a feature with Icon Films.